MY FIANCÉE PROMOTION

EMMY GRAYSON

PRESENTS

Recycling programs for this product may not exist in your area.

ISBN-13: 978-1-335-21388-4

My Fiancée Promotion

Harlequin Enterprises ULC
22 Adelaide St. West, 41st Floor
Toronto, Ontario M5H 4E3, Canada
www.Harlequin.com

HarperCollins Publishers
Macken House, 39/40 Mayor Street Upper,
Dublin 1, D01 C9W8, Ireland
www.HarperCollins.com

Printed in Lithuania

Sera stares at the newspaper with horror etched onto her face.

“What...who took that?”

“One of the event photographers. Once they realized who I was, they decided to make a quick buck.” I toss the newspaper down on the coffee table on top of a stack of books.

She sighs, her hands coming up to her temples. “The damage is done. I’ll submit my resignation on Monday.”

Knots form in my chest, tighten. “No.”

No, only something drastic will repair this.

A frown draws her dark golden brows together. “Then...I don’t understand. What can we do?”

Something stirs inside me at her use of the word *we*. I may not know the woman standing in front of me like I thought I did, but her dedication to Hawke Financial is one thing I don’t doubt.

The one thing I’m counting on.

“I do have a proposal.”

“Okay.” She nods, blows out a harsh breath. “Okay. What do we do.”

“We get engaged.”

A dazzling new trilogy from Harlequin Presents author Emmy Grayson.

Forbidden Bosses

Office-hours temptation, after-hours desire...

Aiden, Dominic and Cassian Hawke: brothers by choice and circumstance if not by blood. All were adopted as boys by their NYC financier father with chips on their shoulders and given a second chance. None of them took that for granted, all three saw it as their life's mission to honor his legacy to them.

Now, they command respect and admiration wherever they go. Their own billion-dollar empires forces to be reckoned with.

They have everything: money, power, passion. Everything...except love! Find out more in...

Aiden & Sera's story
My Fiancée Promotion
Available now!

And look out for Dominic's & Cassian's stories, coming soon!

When **Emmy Grayson** came across her mother's copy of *A Rose in Winter* by Kathleen E. Woodiwiss, she snuck it into her room and promptly fell in love with romance. Over twenty years later, Harlequin Presents made her dream come true by offering her a contract for her first book. When she isn't writing, she's chasing her kids, attempting to garden or carving out a little time on her front porch with her own romance hero.

Books by Emmy Grayson

Harlequin Presents

Diamonds of the Rich and Famous

Prince's Forgotten Diamond

The Diamond Club

Stranded and Seduced

Brides for Greek Brothers

Deception at the Altar
Still the Greek's Wife
Pregnant Behind the Veil

Red-Hot Icelandic Nights

Enemy in His Boardroom
Wed for the Headlines

Visit the Author Profile page
at Harlequin.com for more titles.

To Mom, Dad, and Nate for loving me
through my own hard choices

To John, for loving me as I am

To those who have experienced domestic violence,
you are enough. You are not alone.

CHAPTER ONE

Aiden

THE WOMAN WALKS toward the lake, her eyes fixed on the opposite shore. Barefoot, dark hair pulled back into a braid that trails down her back, a red rose tucked behind her ear. When she glances to the side, I catch a glimpse of the black mask covering half her face.

Most likely one of the performers hired for the Hudson Springs Botanical Gardens' annual "Enchanted Evening" gala. Unlike the glittering gowns and custom-tailored tuxedos sported by the guests, she's dressed simply in a scarlet halter top that stops mid-back and a long black skirt.

I noticed her a few minutes ago inspecting a large metal ring near the bank of the lake. Or rather I noticed her long legs first when the slits in her skirt parted and gave me a tantalizing view of bare skin. It's been nine months since my last affair ended, almost as long since I've enjoyed looking at a woman so much. Her confident yet graceful movements as she walked the length of the catwalk piqued my interest. So, too, did the way she hung back from the group working around the metal ring.

I recognize myself in her, that need for solitude amid

the chaos of a crowded gala. I spent years on the streets of New York City, surrounded by the incessantly shouting people, honking horns and the near-constant shriek of sirens. I can handle a crowd, especially when it's business. But I prefer the quiet of my own company, having complete control of my environment.

The woman stops just a foot away from the water. There's something in the way she stands, the tilt of her chin, that startles me.

Seraphina.

I tense. What the hell is wrong with me? Seraphina Clark has been my executive assistant for the past three years. She's calm, professional, kind. She wears flared skirts with blouses that tie at the neck, and long, slim dresses. Aside from a single plant and one photo of her and her parents, her office is streamlined and immaculate. We may not talk much about our personal lives, but she would have mentioned if she'd taken up fire dancing.

I shift in my seat. I don't like admitting that I noticed her during our interview. A heart-shaped face that reminded me of one of the starlets from the old black-and-white movies my mother used to watch. High cheekbones, a slight point to her chin, and big gray eyes framed by dark lashes that contrasted with the gold color of her hair. Full mouth with that slight curve in her upper lip.

A curve I dreamed about kissing the night I met her. I woke up with a hard cock and shoulder muscles bunched so tight I half wondered if they'd snap.

I almost didn't hire her. But her double major in finance and economics with a minor in PR plus several years of experience working for a financial public relations firm made her the best candidate. I buried my attraction and hired her. Now I can't envision Hawke Financial without her. I've kept my lust in check and she's continued to thrive. The calendars are organized, files are pristine, and my clients are happy.

My jaw tightens. I *was* keeping my lust in check. But my awareness of her has surged in recent months. The click of her heels on the floor kicks my pulse up a notch. The scent of her perfume, light and floral, lingers every time she leaves my office.

My gaze drifts back to the woman in the mask. The full moon streaks her hair with silver. Poised yet relaxed, she's in her own world. So far tonight I've seen an aerialist performing from silks hanging from the branch of a tree, declined to have my future foretold by a fortune teller, and watched a dancing violinist dressed as a wood nymph. Is she performing? Part of the crew?

I watch the woman for one more moment. And then I look away. When I enter into an affair, I do so with calculation. A woman who runs in my social circles, who won't be coming to me for money or, God forbid, a ring. Someone who understands our relationship will have an expiration date. I learned early on that letting myself care too deeply leads to pain. An abusive father who drove my mother to run away to New York City with my brother, David, and me. Then Mom passing. David and I split up into different foster homes. Me taking to the streets after my foster father hit me one too many times.

After all that, I should have learned my lesson. But maybe my falling in with Dominic after he offered me a tent in a trash-strewn alley in East Harlem softened me. He took me in, gave me a home, taught me how to pick pockets and survive. We had each other's backs, then Cassian's when we added him to our group. For the first time in a long time, I let down my guard. Started to hope again.

Until Melanie took what little bit of heart I had left and ground it into dust.

I will never make the mistake of falling in love again. If Seraphina wasn't off-limits for being my employee, she'd be off-limits for being the exact opposite of what I look for in my relationships. She's made it easier by never being anything but the consummate professional. Not one teasing comment, not one flirtatious glance. She even insists on calling me Mr. Hawke, even though I've invited her to call me Aiden on multiple occasions. I'd be mildly irritated by her lack of response if it didn't make it easier to keep her at a distance.

Fire flares up from the metal ring standing upright on the banks of the lake. The crowd collectively gasps. A few squeal like they're kids at a carnival instead of a gala. I watch the flames burn for a minute. When I glance back at the edge of the lake, the woman is gone.

I swirl the ice in my glass. Of all the events I've attended, this is the strangest. The five hundred acres of New York's finest flowers and plants are lit by torches and flickering solar lights tucked beneath leaves and petals, creating an admittedly charming glow. Lanterns float on the surface of the lake. The raised wooden terrace I'm lounging on is cordoned off with a red velvet rope, with plush chairs and couches arranged beneath strings of golden lights. Waiters pass through the crowd below with silver platters bearing either flutes of champagne or hors d'oeuvres like edible flower spring rolls with ginger sauce and lavender-scented chicken skewers.

A world I never imagined possible for someone who

grew up like I did. It's been twenty years since Cassian got caught picking the pocket of a man with silver hair that reminded me of a lion's mane. Dominic and I sprung into action, determined to rescue Cassian from the man's grip. Instead, the man made us an offer: He could call the police officer who was standing half a block away or he could buy us dinner. I wanted nothing to do with him. But it was winter, food was scarce, and tourists with thick wallets even scarcer.

I never imagined that dinner at one of the nicest restaurants in Midtown, where the concierge greeted our host and his three dirty guests like we were royalty, would eventually lead to us being formally adopted by one of the most renowned private equity titans in the world. A man worth billions who took us in because he admired our loyalty to each other and wanted to give us a chance, the same way someone had given him an opportunity when he'd been down on his luck.

Regret tries to creep in. I never fully let John in, even after all he did for me. But I don't dwell on what I might have done differently before his unexpected passing a few years ago. He gave me a chance at a new life simply because he could. Even if I didn't open up emotionally, I made my appreciation known, dedicated myself to doing the most with the chance he gave me.

My eyes flick to the older man sitting in the plush chair to my right in the cordoned-off VIP section. I've gotten used to success. But now I'm facing down a true challenge, one with repercussions far more dangerous than simply losing money. The man next to me is the key, if only he'd stop dragging his feet and accept my recommendation.

George Randolph worked his way up from a logger in the Catskills to owning his own lumber mill, then pivoting to sustainable building materials and a side business in forest tourism that's netted him millions. Millions he's chosen to have me manage as his personal financial advisor through my firm, Hawke Financial. Investing in the hedge fund I established, too, has made him my most important client.

Like me, the man lives and breathes work. I'm used to seeing him in a suit and tie with his steel gray hair combed back and a razor-sharp expression on his thick face. Tonight, however, he's dressed in a navy tuxedo, complete with a bow tie that matches his wife's gown. A faint smile lingers at the corners of his mouth. He looks relaxed. Almost happy.

Which is exactly where I need him if I'm going to sell him on my latest proposal for his portfolio. After I grew his portfolio by 42 percent the first year, Randolph has replied "Yes" to every recommendation I've made.

But not my last one. Not the most important advice I've ever given.

"Better than last year's performers," Randolph says with a nod to the burning ring. "Opera singers." He shudders. "Torture."

My lips twitch. "I'm surprised, given your wife's patronage of the New York City Opera."

Randolph's bushy eyebrows shoot up. "Surprised you remember."

I don't take it as an insult. Anyone who knows me, even on a cursory level, would not describe me as personable. I recall personal details easily thanks to Seraphina. The woman has a steel-trap for a mind, one that captures the kind of details I don't always pay attention to. I prefer facts, numbers, figures. Things I can predict, control. Seraphina isn't just good with finances, but with people, too. She maintains dossiers on all of my clients and updates them with stunning efficiency. If someone gets married, has a child, earns a promotion, loses a loved one, or experiences some other milestone, it goes in their file. Details like how Randolph's logging days working alongside prisoners formed his views on prison reform, including a strong distaste for for-profit prison.

I take a long sip of my gin and tonic. The crisp floral notes of the gin, tempered by the bubbling tonic water, keeps my anger banked every time I think of New Field Penitentiary. Achieving a hostile takeover of the private jail would give Randolph a strong foundation for his stance on prison reform if he's elected as senator this fall. And the polls are favorable.

The deal, however, isn't just for my client. It will give me great satisfaction orchestrating the downfall of the current sadistic owner of New Field. Victor Hale, man who prioritizes profit over the people under his care. A man who looked the other way as my biological brother, David, was kept in solitary confinement for days without food or medical treatment for the broken leg he'd sustained during a prison riot. Who threatened to trot David's record out for public viewing and ruin his life if I went to the press.

I wait until the anger and guilt bleed out before releasing a pent-up breath. David's safe now. He's doing better. If I'm going to do this for him, for us, I need to stay sharp, focused. It's not just enough to punish Hale. New Field needs to be taken over by someone who will turn it around and make sure it's run ethically. Someone who believes in prison reform.

Someone like George Randolph.

"I proposed to Martine here. It's been years since we've been back." Randolph glances around, that same faint smile on his face. "When are you going to settle down?"

One long sip of my drink gives me time to prepare my answer. My last relationship ended in a messier fashion than I'm accustomed to. But it's not just that, I grudgingly admit. My interest in dating has waned. I'm not wanting marriage or anything binding. But the quick, intense flings are no longer satisfying.

"I'm not looking to settle at this time."

Randolph huffs. "After that debacle with your actress, I'd think you'd be looking for something more…solid."

I keep my face smooth even though I want to scowl. Ever since Randolph decided to run for Senate, he's been mentioning my dating life more and more.

"We'll see."

Randolph runs a hand over his mouth. "Look, Hawke, part of the reason I asked you here tonight was to tell you I'm seriously considering the New Field deal."

Triumph surges in my chest, but I tamp it down. This is the closest I've gotten so far, but we're nowhere close to signing.

"I'm glad to hear it."

"However," he continues in a tone that has me mentally prepping for whatever bomb he's about to drop, "my public relations team has concerns about my continuing to work with Hawke Financial."

I still. "Oh?"

"I'm running against a popular candidate. If you were to have another incident like in October—"

I frown. "Kacey Delamare and I broke up. That's it."

"And she referenced you in interviews for months," Randolph replies. "Spilled private details. Every time you're seen with a woman, it turns into a media frenzy."

I stare at him. I've made this man millions of dollars, supported his candidacy. Now he's going to cut me loose because I like to date?

If I didn't need him, I'd tell him to go to hell.

"What do you want from me, Randolph? I haven't dated anyone in nearly a year," I add.

"No, but the reputation lingers. If you were to date a woman longer than two months, that would be a step in the right direction. Something more permanent would be preferable." Randolph stands. "I'm going to grab one of those tiny things they call a plate and fill it with as much food as I can, and then track down my wife. Would you like to join me?"

No. I have zero interest in being anywhere near George Randolph right now. Not with the word *permanent* ringing in my ears. I gesture toward the stage by the lake. "I'm going to watch a few more of the performances."

"Suit yourself." He starts down the stairs, then pauses and looks back at me. "I want this to work, Hawke."

I nod. "I'll consider what you said."

I wait until Randolph disappears into the crowd before I pull out my phone and text Seraphina. I try not to contact her outside of working hours. But she knows Randolph, knows the New Field deal inside and out. I want her perspective on this.

Entering into a long-term relationship makes me want

to order another two or three gin and tonics. But it might be the only thing that will keep Randolph with Hawke Financial. The only thing that will get him to agree to the New Field deal.

Several minutes pass as an acrobat and then a magician perform on the catwalk. I glance at my phone, then frown when the screen remains dark. I don't require Seraphina to be available on the weekends. Not unless we have something critical happening. But she usually replies within a couple minutes.

She could have gone to bed early, I remind myself. Maybe she's attending an event in the city. Maybe she's on a date.

The last thought is not a pleasant one.

My frowns deepens. This is why I prefer to keep people at arm's length. It doesn't do anyone any favors to get attached, even if the attachment is rooted in respect and professional appreciation. Emotions eventually cloud one's judgment, loosen one's grip on control. Let in the kind of pain you're not sure you can survive.

Two faces slip into my consciousness. Mom lying in the hospital, pale and lifeless, the incessant beeping of the heart monitor slipping into one long, mournful tone. David clutching on to my arm as the social worker tried to wrestle him into the car that would take him to a different foster home. Me promising him I would find him, would make us a family again as his hot tears scalded my skin.

Fuck.

I'm revisiting my past more with the New Field deal looming over me. But God, I hate it. It yanks me outside the walls I crafted years ago to keep people and all the pain they bring with them out. I make very few exceptions to venturing past my own boundaries or letting people in.

My eyes drop down to my phone again. Where the hell is she?

The music stops. The lights dim, save for the lanterns drifting across the lake and the ring of fire burning by the water.

A figure walks onto the catwalk that runs from the shore through the fiery ring. The woman from the lake. Her head is bowed, her hair now wrapped into a low bun. In one hand is a long stick. That sense of recognition pulls at me again, but I ignore it.

Faint notes dance through the speakers, like the keys of a piano with an electric undercurrent. She raises her head and walks forward to the ring with elegant strides. She raises one end of the stick to the flames. It flares, catches fire. Then she reaches up, touches her hand to the heat. Fire flickers in her palm as she touches the other end of the staff. I don't know why, but the sight of flames in her hand is sexy as hell.

Her body freezes. Time stands still as a hush steals over the crowd. My chest tightens.

The violin cuts through the night, a sharp melody perfectly timed with the fire dancer's sudden leap into the air. My blood thickens as she lands, raises the fiery staff and then rolls it down with expert precision. The burning ends hit the ground. Fire shoots up, races down the catwalk in twin lines. The dancer spins, twirls, leaps between them in time to the music. She pauses every few steps to spin the staff around her neck, roll it down her arms, toss it in the air and catch it. Every move is perfectly choreographed, hypnotic and primal.

I sit, rooted to the spot, as she dances to the end of the catwalk. She tosses the flaming staff to a man standing off to the side, who tosses her what looks like a sword. She dips the tip into the fire and the entire blade turns to flame. The music crescendos as she spins, the sword creating a circle of sparks around her.

She stops. Whips the sword above her head and holds it as the music fades, replaced by thunderous applause. I stare, mesmerized, as she artfully spins the sword in her hand before taking a bow. She straightens.

And looks right at me.

Lust strikes like a lightning bolt as we stare at each other across the crowd. Electricity arcs between us, pulses like a heartbeat. I want her. I want to know her name, want to see the face beneath the mask. Need her in my bed, beneath me, surrounding me.

The eyes behind the mask widen, bottle green and suddenly filled with fear. Her lips part, and even though she's a stone's throw away, I can read the name she utters.

My name.

Recognition punches through the desire, lets in a tidal wave of shock.

Seraphina.

Seraphina turns to the still-applauding crowd, bows and straightens. She doesn't look in my direction again. No, she turns, walks back through fiery ring, hands her sword to someone, and quickly walks away along the shores of the lake into the darkness.

Runs away.

I surge to my feet, passing my glass to a surprised waitress as I hurry down the stairs. Why is my mild-mannered, incredibly reliable executive assistant dancing around with a sword she lit on fire? How long has she been doing this?

Worse, how the hell am I going to be able to be around her now? After seeing her dance so sensually, seeing her long bare legs and the way that top cupped her breasts—

I stop my train of thought and focus on easing my way through the crowd. I don't know what I'm going to do or say when I find Seraphina. But I need to see her, need to talk to her.

I finally spy the footpath, a narrow span of dirt near the water's edge. I plunge down the path, driven by a compulsion I should be fighting but can no longer resist.

CHAPTER TWO

Seraphina

Oh my God, what have I done?

I jog down the path hugging the edge of the lake, trying to keep my pace steady and my shoulders relaxed in case anyone else from Cirque Obsidian is watching me. They know my first name, know that I work for a big finance firm in the city. But otherwise, I keep my personal details private. My dancing is a part of me I don't like to share.

Except my boss just saw me dressed in the equivalent of a bikini top and a skirt that barely does its job.

I glance back at the fire ring. Even after a year of fire dancing, the sight of the flames sends a jolt of energy spiraling through me. Empowering yet also humbling. Without practice, commitment, dedication, I could very easily get burned.

Much like working with Aiden Hawke.

My breath rushes out. When I finished my performance and locked eyes with Aiden, I froze. Something pulsed between us, a split-second heat that had nothing to do with the fire blazing just behind me.

Stupid.

My breathing slowly steadies as I move farther away from the gathering. I'm still painfully aware of every slam of my heart against my ribs. But even with the shock of encountering Aiden, I wouldn't change my decision to dance tonight. How could I turn down the woman who helped me reclaim not just my confidence and my self-esteem but ownership over my own body?

The shrill ring of a phone at five o'clock this morning sent fear rushing through me when I saw Jessica King's name on the screen, the owner of Cirque Obsidian. But when I'd answered, her excitement burst through the phone as she informed me her sister had gone into labor a month early and they were en route to the hospital. With her brother-in-law deployed overseas and her parents living in Oregon, Jessica was going to be her sister's birthing partner.

Which had left the Hudson Springs Botanical Gardens without a fire dancer for their luxurious gala. With Jessica's other fire dancers performing back in the city, there had been no one left to perform. Even as nerves fluttered like butterflies in my stomach, I already knew my answer. It was Jessica who helped me take those first steps toward reclaiming myself after years of living under Brett Sinclair's thumb. After I finally mustered the courage to leave him, fleeing in the dark with nothing but the clothes on my back, I found my way to Grace's Refuge. The shelter not only gave me a place to stay while I put my life back together, but when my advocate learned I used to dance before letting Brett pressure me to stop, she introduced me to Jessica. I can't imagine my life without Obsidian.

* * *

Dancing always makes me feel…sensual. Sexy. Even though I'd been so nervous to take the stage tonight, I was riding high at the end. Making eye contact with my hot boss was unexpected. Any emotions I experienced were one-sided. Aiden might have appreciated my performance, but there's no way he felt the same, sudden slam of desire I did. The man is cool and calculating, even when it comes to the numerous relationships he's had since I started working for him.

Yet the way he'd sat up, shoulders back, his attention laser-focused on me, had sent a thrilling jolt through me. One quickly followed by a cold, heavy dose of reality that sent me fleeing.

He didn't recognize you. He didn't see you.

I repeat the comforting phrases in my mind. I've had a slight crush on my boss ever since he hired me. Crush, not love. The last time I thought I was in love, it nearly broke me.

Admiring Aiden, enjoying the sight of his sculpted cheekbones and the tiny dimple that flashes on very rare occasions just above the razor-straight line of his jaw, engaging in intelligent conversations with someone who respects me, are all things I can enjoy while maintaining my distance. He sees me as a qualified employee, nothing more. Still, I always call him Mr. Hawke, a small reminder to myself that he's my boss and very much off-limits.

Besides, I love working for Hawke Financial. Aiden's demanding, but fair. He gave me a chance and has continuously given me more intricate and detailed assignments. I liked what I did at the financial PR firm I worked for before I landed the job at Hawke Financial, but I've fallen in love with my role: the research, the numbers, the analyses and trying to predict outcomes of the perpetually changing markets.

Not only do I love my job, but I had planned on asking for Aiden's help on Monday. Mona, the director of Grace's Refuge, sent an email this morning to staff and volunteers letting us know they were looking for a new building. Their sleazy landlord had doubled their rent with hopes of running them off and selling his property to clamoring developers. Aiden and his adopted brothers run a foundation that disperses money for causes exactly like this.

But I need to make sure things are okay between us on Monday, confirm that he didn't recognize me. Once I have that reassurance, I'll ask about Grace's Refuge.

I stop underneath the sweeping branches of a willow tree and stare out over the lake. Given Aiden's well-known past as a pickpocket during his teenage years, I don't think he'd care one way or the other what I do with my time outside of work. But dancing…it's mine. I wore the brunette wig and mask for me. I wanted to do this for Jessica, but I'm not ready to share both my dancing and myself. Not yet. Tonight, however, was still supposed to be a big moment. Another step in my healing journey, inching closer to finally letting my guard down and maybe, just maybe, working my way up to opening my heart again.

Instead, I nearly dropped my sword and then took off like a coward.

I look up at the night sky, at the smattering of stars scattered across the black. Sometimes it seems like yesterday when I nearly broke down in the courtroom as a judge found my ex-boyfriend Brett Sinclair guilty of domestic battery, harassment and interstate violation of the restraining order I filed against him, and sentenced him to twenty-five years in prison. Other days it feels far longer than four years ago, like looking through a foggy mirror and trying to determine if that really happened or if it was just a horrible nightmare.

I breathe in deeply, then slowly exhale. Brett's in jail, and will be for years before he's eligible for parole. I volunteer at Grace's once a week, doing what I can to give back to the shelter that opened its doors to me when I was so low I thought there was no way I could claw my way back up. And now, because of them, I have a thriving career and a passion that's given me back my confidence, my power.

And there's the thrill of taking the subway to Bushwick on Wednesday and Saturday nights to practice at Obsidian's studio inside a converted warehouse, mingling with fellow dancers, trapeze artists and gymnasts. After living my life to meet someone else's preferences, the freedom is intoxicating, as is the secrecy.

Should I have told Aiden about Cirque Obsidian? The dancing?

No. Not only is it mine to share, but Aiden has always maintained strict professional boundaries. Occasionally he'll ask how my weekend was, but that's the extent of our personal talk. What I know of his life outside the office comes from biographies written up in the *Wall Street Journal* or splashy tabloid photos speculating whether he's dating this tech entrepreneur or that neurosurgeon. He doesn't have an interest in me outside of work, which makes it easy to keep my emotions in check.

I glance out over the water. My crush on Aiden isn't just because of his long, sculpted face or deep-set brown eyes. His intelligence, his commitment to the firm he built, the cool respect he gives everyone in equal measure, are what keep me in a slight state of awe. That and how he talks to me like I'm his equal, how he asks for my insight and trusts my opinions on his clients, their motivations. No one's ever valued my opinion as much as one of the wealthiest hedge fund founders and most respected personal financial advisors in the world.

Although, I admit with a small smile as I resume walking, him being sexy as hell certainly doesn't hurt. I only dated a couple guys before I became involved with Brett. None of them had the same commanding presence, the same sheer force when they simply walked into a room, as Aiden Hawke does.

I don't know why he's here. It was definitely not on his calendar when I left work yesterday. Maybe he's here on a date.

Which is none of your concern, I remind myself firmly even as my stomach sinks.

I glance back over my shoulder. The fire ring burns brightly in the darkness, but I must have walked nearly a quarter of a mile. The music is faint, overridden by the chorus of frogs and occasional trill of a night bird. Moonlight sparkles on the water of the lake. A light summer breeze brushes over my skin.

I have one dance left, and then I'm done. I'm not looking forward to the long drive home, but there will be a glass of wine and my current book waiting for me.

A twig snaps in the darkness. Fear explodes inside me, takes over and roots my feet to the ground. My breathing quickens as my heart pounds against my chest in painful thuds.

Probably a guest. Maybe a couple sneaking away for a kiss. But there's no murmured voices, no dim glow of a phone or flashlight.

The past rears up. Brett, eyes hard and furious, a bottle in his hand as he raises it above his head. A soft whimper rises to my lips.

Steady, Seraphina.

I mentally grab on to my fear, shove it down. I'm stronger, prepared. I keep my feet planted but crouch, loosening my knees as I wait. Listen for the next quiet sound of a footstep whispering across the grass. Wait until I sense someone just behind me.

I whirl. My left arm comes up, blocking my face as my right hand punches out. Fingers curl around my wrist and yank me forward. My heart shoots into my throat as I'm spun around and yanked against a hard chest.

You're a weapon, Seraphina.

I stomp down on a foot. The grunt of pain in my ear energizes me. I whip my head back, wince as I connect with my attacker's face. The grip on my wrist loosens and I dart forward, prepared to run.

"Damn it, Seraphina, did you take up boxing, too?"

I freeze. My heart is pounding so hard it takes a moment for the voice to penetrate.

Oh no.

My fear evaporates, replaced by cold, bone-deep panic of a different nature. Slowly, I turn.

Aiden stands just a couple feet away. Silver light streaks his thick, dark brown hair, highlights the cut of his cheekbones and caresses his strong jaw.

It also shows off the blood trickling down from his lower lip.

"Oh, God."

I reach up to wipe the blood away, then snatch my hand away as his eyes narrow.

"Mr. Hawke. I'm so sorry. Is…is your nose broken?"

He reaches up and runs a finger down the bridge of his nose. The almost imperceptible wince reignites my guilt, leaving me swallowing the bitterness in my mouth.

"Despite your impressive efforts, no, it's not." He lowers his chin. "You shouldn't be out here alone."

The growl in his voice erases some of my panic, although the chauvinistic tone grates on my nerves.

"Perhaps," I reply. "But you shouldn't be sneaking around in the dark."

One dark eyebrow arches up. A traitorous thrill shoots through me. Even with blood on his chin, he's still too handsome for his own good. The faint cleft in his chin, the square jaw, the regal elegance contrasted by his broad shoulders and towering height.

"I wasn't sneaking."

I bite down on my lower lip to stifle a smile. He sounds so insulted.

"Then why didn't you call out?"

"You're wearing a mask and either a wig or you dyed your hair." He leans in to peer at the synthetic fiber wig I borrowed from Jessica, bringing him closer and making my breath hitch. "Given the effort you put into concealing your identity, I didn't think you'd like me calling out your name in case someone else is exploring."

Okay, fair point.

His eyes flicker down to my halter top and skirt. My

chest constricts as I force myself to keep my arms at my sides instead of crossing them over my breasts or pulling the fabric of my skirt over my legs.

His gaze snaps back up to my face, eyes cold and hard. I barely resist the urge to gulp as I force myself to lift my chin.

"Do we have a problem, Mr. Hawke?"

"Oh, we most certainly do, Miss Clark."

He takes a step toward me. I stand my ground. Barely.

"How long have you been doing this?"

I narrow my eyes. I most definitely do not like his tone.

"Well, I got here about six o'clock—"

"That's not what I mean," Aiden snaps, "and you know it."

"About a year," I bite out. "Not that it's any of your business what I do outside of working hours."

"You've been doing…this," he says with a wave back toward the fire ring, "and never told me?"

Confused, I frown. "Why would I? You've always touted professional is separate from personal."

"This is different, Seraphina."

I blink. I never imagined Aiden would find out my secret. But somehow, I thought if it ever did come to life, he would understand. I know he ran away from foster care when he was barely thirteen, that he used less than legal means to survive. He's crafted a new life for himself. An incredible career. Yet here he is, looking down his nose at me. Hurt pulses through me, ice-cold and sharp. I let it live for a moment, mentally store it as a reminder for what happens when you let your guard down.

And then I do what I learned how to do when the going gets tough; I shut off my emotions until there's nothing but a blissful numbness, a void that allows me to move forward in the moment.

"I'm up in a few minutes. We can talk Monday."

I start to pass by. He reaches out and grabs my wrist again. The heat of his fingers sears my skin as I tense. *No, no, no.* Now is not the time for my stupid crush to show its face. He's my boss. Not my friend. Not my lover.

He reaches out, places his hand on my shoulder and turns me to face him. My breath catches as his bare palms lie flat against my skin.

"Damn it, Seraphina, I don't care how you spend your personal time. I just…" His voice drifts off. "You go to greenhouses and music festivals and bookstores on weekends."

I blink, surprised he knows these details about me. "And?"

"So, I didn't think my executive assistant was out playing with fire on her nights off."

I smile slightly. "I'm not playing with fire, Mr. Hawke. I wield it."

Something flares in his eyes. It's too dark to tell what. Probably anger, although why he's upset, I have no idea.

He blinks. Breathes in. His eyes drop down to my lips. I suck in a shocked breath at the sudden flare in his eyes. Can it be possible that Aiden feels something for me? Even if it's just simple lust, the idea is tempting, intoxicating.

He leans down. My lips part.

A shriek rents the air. A ball of light arcs up from the far side of the lake into the sky, then explodes into a shower of gold and red sparks.

Fireworks, I realize, as reality settles back in. I take

a huge step back. Aiden releases his grip on my wrist. My heart is pounding, my breath building up in my chest until it comes out in a rush. Aiden's staring at me like he's never seen me before.

Or, worse, like he's seeing everything I've fought to conceal. Like he's seeing me.

The panic I experienced earlier is nothing compared to the full-blown terror that surges up my throat and fills my veins with a frantic humming. I don't want Aiden looking at me like this. Before tonight, I was a dependable employee with an admirable track record.

Now he's looking at me like…like a man looks at a woman he wants. And God help me, my body is responding in a way it hasn't in years.

No, I admit as my breathing turns shallow. Never. I've never felt this before, this desire that sinks into my bones. Each blaze of heat flickering across my skin is more seductive than any dance I've performed.

Far more dangerous than anything I've ever done with fire dancing.

I step back farther, needing the physical distance to rein in my chaotic thoughts. I can't imagine not working for Aiden, not analyzing market analyses and client profiles, reconciling the two as he and I discuss the potential routes and recommendations. But how can I continue working for him after this? After he's gotten a glimpse behind the walls that have kept me safe for years?

"If necessary, I'll submit my resignation on Monday."

His eyes widen. His lips part, as if he's about to retort, but I brush past him and walk back down the path.

I have one performance left. I'll need to be careful. I'm upset, out-of-sorts. That's when mistakes happen, when performers get burned. I'll take my performance down a notch.

And then I'm going to go home, opening a bottle of merlot, and not talk to anyone else for the rest of the weekend.

Especially Aiden Hawke.

CHAPTER THREE

Aiden

Cool air chills the water droplets clinging to my skin as I haul myself out of the pool. I sit on the edge, my calves still submerged, my breathing harsh. My blood is pumping, heart racing as I stare at the rippling water.

For a precious thirty minutes, there was nothing but the water and me. No thoughts of Seraphina, no memories of how she felt in my arms, no faint gasp echoing in my ears as her eyes met mine.

My fingers tighten on the edge of the pool. In three years, I've never once seen Seraphina so much as give me a flirtatious glance. But last night, if I'd lowered my mouth to hers, there's no doubt in my mind she would have kissed me back.

Blood rushes to my cock as images fill my mind. The sensuous twist of her hips as she spun, the way her skirt parted to show her bare legs as she leaped with fire in her hands.

Legs I can easily picture wrapped around my waist as I slide deep inside her.

Fuck.

I stand and stalk across the terrace to the chaise longue where I tossed my water bottle and towel. I flip open the lid and chug the entire bottle. As I grab the towel and wrap it around my hips, I stare out over Central Park. It's just six o'clock in the morning. Mist clings to the trees over a thousand feet below me. The sun's already broken the horizon but is still hidden behind the sweep of skyscrapers and mammoth structures that make up New York City.

One of my favorite times of the day, when the city is the closest to quiet it will ever get. When I can stand and take it all in, look down on the streets that once treated me with such disdain, and know that I now stand above.

But there's no pride this morning, no satisfaction. Instead, there's lust. Obsession. Three years of suppressing my attraction for Seraphina, all that effort erased by my carelessness.

I turn my back on the city and walk through the terrace doors into my penthouse just in time to hear the shrill ring of my phone. I frown as I walk toward the kitchen. Who the hell is calling me just after sunrise on a Sunday morning?

Seraphina.

No. Judging by the way she ran last night after dropping her bombshell comment about resigning, I'm the last person she wants to talk to now. Although I should probably text her today and disabuse her of that notion. I don't fault her for thinking the worst. I didn't exactly do a good job of explaining why I followed her or why I was upset.

Hell, I could barely figure it out myself. I normally have an iron grip on myself. But when our eyes met, when

I realized who the seductive fire dancer was, I had to follow her. Had to talk to her, demand answers.

Instead, I nearly made the mistake of a lifetime.

I'll fix this, one way or another. It might take a generous bump in pay or an extra vacation, but I will do whatever it takes to keep Seraphina at Hawke Financial.

The phone stops ringing as I near the kitchen, only to immediately squawk again seconds later. I grab it from where I laid it next to the coffeepot. I read the name on the screen and frown.

"Morning, Randolph. Everything okay?"

"What the hell do you think, Hawke?"

Randolph's furious words snap across the line. Irritation takes hold. I wait a moment, breathe in then out, get a hold on my anger before I answer.

"Judging by the early hour and your tone, I'd say not okay."

"Damn right!" Randolph's voice vibrates with anger. "I trusted you, damn it, and this is how you repay me?"

I open one of the cabinet doors and reach for a mug. Whatever's eating him will require a huge cup of coffee.

"Repay you how, Randolph?"

"You and Seraphina!"

I nearly drop the mug. Slowly, I lower it to the counter, turn and lean against it as the alarm takes hold, builds until it's flowing through my veins like a flood.

"What are you talking about?" I keep my tone even, calm.

"The pictures are everywhere, Hawke. Both of you at the gala last night."

I put Randolph on speaker and quickly pull up my news app. I type in my name and three seconds later I see it.

Or rather them, as there are several photos of Seraphina and me next to the lake. One is of us talking, Seraphina's mouth twisted into a scowl beneath the mask. The second is of her starting to walk past me.

But it's the third that's the most damning. My hands on her shoulders, my head lowered, her staring up at me from behind the mask. The headlines are just as bad, from Fire Dancer Seduces Billionaire Boss, to Playboy Financier's Secret Affair with His Own Secretary!

I swear under my breath.

"Well, Hawke?"

Randolph's voice fills the kitchen. Gone is the jovial grandfather figure who drank cocktails with me by the lake just a few hours ago. In his place is the hard-line CEO who wields considerable power and influence over this city, who brought me over a dozen new clients over the last few years.

If Randolph cuts ties with Hawke Financial, we'd survive. I've made enough wealthy people even wealthier that even if he were to intentionally try to ruin me, he'd fail.

New Field.

My hand tightens on my phone. I need Randolph. Yes, there are other ways of getting to New Field. But ways that will cost more time and don't have near the same chance of success.

I stare down at Seraphina's face. At her parted lips, the way her body leans in toward mine. A picture of secret lovers finally caught.

The answer is right in front of me. Not just the answer to potentially stop Randolph's tirade in my ear, but to address his concerns from last night, to satisfy his obsession with monogamous commitment as I push him one step closer toward the New Field takeover. Turning the tide of scandalous press and using it to my advantage will be an added bonus.

Resolution falls into place with the strength of tumblers in a lock. I don't like lying to Randolph, just like I don't like the idea of a supposed engagement with the woman I've been fighting my attraction to for three years. But my mother didn't like working three jobs to keep a roof over our heads. My brother didn't like being sent to a prison that prioritized punishment over retribution. If I'm truly going to have my revenge, it will require sacrifice.

Seraphina's not going to be happy. But she cares about New Field. She'll see reason. Even if she's furious, I'll write her a check so large it would pacify anyone.

I take my phone off speaker. Press it to my ear. Inhale deeply.

Then leap.

"Seraphina and I are engaged."

Seraphina

The brisk knock on my door jerks me out of my meditative state. I curse as I teeter in Revolved Half-Moon Pose, then fall flat on my butt.

I sigh. I spent all night tossing and turning, memories of my near kiss with my boss and nightmares of being fired randomly jerking me out of sleep until I finally gave up around six. I made myself a cup of tea, only to spill half of it across the counter as I read a text from Mona, the director of Grace's Refuge. The landlord had given them until next month to come up with the money. But she was already anticipating having to temporarily shut down while they hunted for a new space.

After I cleaned up the tea, I rolled out my yoga mat and slipped into the one thing guaranteed to relax me. The sequence of poses, monitoring my breathing, focusing on my body in the moment, all of it helped me in the months after the trial. It was my first foray into regaining control of my body and my mind.

Apparently, the universe is going to deny me even that simple pleasure today.

Another knock, this one louder and more insistent, has me growling at the door.

"I'm coming!"

I stand up, hands fisted at my sides as I try to summon some kind of patience. I have no idea who is knocking on my door at seven in the morning on a freaking Sunday, but they better have a damn good reason for it.

I put my eye to the peephole…and nearly swallow my tongue.

Aiden's there. Right outside my door.

"I know you're there, Seraphina."

I lean my forehead against the door. Heat burns away the last of my inner peace and replaces it with some of my sordid dreams from the night before. Dreams of Aiden actually kissing me, his hands cupping my breasts, undoing the ties of my top—

I swallow hard. Dreams. They were just dreams. And they'll never be more than dreams. He's probably here to demand an explanation, if not my resignation.

And if he does, I firmly tell myself, *you'll give it to him along with your best wishes to go to hell.*

I've survived far worse things than unemployment. And if Aiden is truly going to hold me to such a ridiculous double standard given his past, then working for him is no longer a good fit for me anyway.

"Open the door, Seraphina."

Slowly, I undo the lock and open the door. And scowl. I'm in a sports bra and leggings, my hair pulled up into the messiest of messy buns. Zero makeup, traces of sweat on my face.

And then there's Aiden Hawke. Face freshly shaven, hair combed back from his broad forehead, sporting a gray blazer and matching pants with a crisp white shirt.

How the hell does the man look this put together on a weekend morning?

"Aid…" I clear my throat. "Good morning, Mr. Hawke."

"Seraphina."

He starts to move forward. I angle my body to block the doorway. A move that sends a clear message that I have no interest in allowing him inside my apartment, but also has the unfortunate effect of bringing us within inches of each other. I know his scent: smoky wood and spicy warmth. But here, with me in a bra and leggings and him so close I can feel the heat of his body, his fragrance is earthier, more sensual.

My hand tightens on the doorframe. His gaze is fathomless, shadowed.

"May I come in?"

I suddenly feel very, very tired. I didn't get home until past midnight. I tossed and turned for hours. And having my boss see me like that…

Fire dancing has given me so much in the past year—confidence, strength, passion. When I dance, I pour myself into every move. Knowing Aiden saw me like that makes me feel raw. Vulnerable. And I hate it.

"Can we talk tomorrow? I'm busy and I…"

My voice trails off as he holds up the newspaper. I stare at it, confused. Then, slowly, I realize what I'm staring at. My lips part, flap uselessly as I try to form words.

Him. Me. Our bodies way too close. And a sordid headline that leaves me hollow.

"What…" So many thoughts rush through my mind I grow dizzy. My hand clamps down so tight on the doorframe I might get splinters. "That's not possible."

"Unfortunately, it is."

Aiden's grim voice breaks through my shock. I tear my eyes away from the grainy photo of us by the lake and focus on him.

"I had nothing to do with—"

"I know that, Seraphina." He glances over his shoulder. "Now let me in before one of the photographers lurking downstairs snaps a photo of us."

My jaw drops. "What?"

"Now."

He barks the word like an order, but he doesn't push his way past me. I register that as I step back and finally let him pass before I close the door and slam the dead bolt into place. I keep staring at the door for far too long. But I need this moment before I face him. Need to get a grip on my racing thoughts, on my pounding heart, on the fear rising up inside me.

Why the hell did I ever agree to dance last night? My life was good. Really good. A job I loved, a boss I respected and, yes, found attractive, but always from a safe distance. I'd found my way back to dancing. Jessica and I are becoming friends. I see my parents every—

My head snaps up and I push off the door.

"I need to call my parents."

I'm halfway across the room when Aiden grabs my arm and stops me.

"We need to talk first."

I whirl around, resisting the urge to shove him away with both hands. This is his fault, too.

"Who took the photo?"

"One of the event photographers. Once they realized who I was, they decided to follow me thinking I was meeting a new lover." He scowls at the paper in his hands. "My best guess is he asked for your name and put two and two together. But he's no longer employed."

My jaw drops. "You had him fired?"

"His job was to photograph the event, not pretend to be a paparazzo. The Gardens agreed with me."

He's got a point. But if he hadn't followed me, if he had just stayed in his VIP booth sipping hundred-dollar cocktails, none of this would have happened.

"Why the hell did you come after me last night?"

I'm risking the future of my job with my tone. But I'm so angry, stripped bare in front of a man I never wanted to be vulnerable in front of. So damn afraid I can barely see straight. Memories of Brett rear up, his face twisted into a mask of such burning anger I can still taste the fear from all those years ago. But I'm not going to cave this time. I will start over from scratch if I have to.

I whirl and jab a finger at Aiden.

"I'm allowed to have a life outside of work, and if you're going to tell me I can't work for you and dance then you can just shove one of your seven-figure contracts up your—"

"Stop."

He barks out the one word with the same ferocity he's used when dealing with cranky clients. My first inclination is to back down, apologize. So I straighten my shoulders, raise my chin and meet his gaze head-on.

"As I said last night, this has nothing to do with your dancing." Aiden runs a hand through his hair. "For God's sake, Seraphina, it's a well-known fact I spent several years picking pockets in New York before John found me. Do you really think I'd judge you for something as mundane as learning how to dance?"

"Maybe not you, but your clients—"

"My clients," he grounds out, "can go to hell if they have a problem with it, especially since I counted at least seven of them in attendance last night thoroughly enjoying the festivities."

My anger drains away as I deflate.

"When you said we have a problem… I thought…"

"I was surprised last night. I wasn't at my most eloquent."

"So why did you come after me?"

One long, slow blink. His tell. I've seen him in enough conferences and on enough phone calls to know he's going to lie, or at the very least only share half the truth.

"I was shocked."

"Shocked?" I repeat.

"Yes, Seraphina, shocked." My six-hundred-square-foot studio apartment shrinks as he takes a step closer. "My prim, proper assistant twirling a stick that's on fire around her head like it couldn't suddenly combust and kill her? Yes," he repeats, his voice hardening, "I was shocked."

I roll my eyes. I had the same conversation with my father when I first started dabbling in fire dancing.

"It won't randomly combust. I use controlled fuel application to the wick ends—"

"Not my point," Aiden snaps. "How would you feel if you had seen me last night walking around on stilts?"

I try to keep a straight face. Try and fail epically as a snort of laughter escapes.

Aiden's eyebrows draw together. "What," he asks through gritted teeth, "is so damned funny?"

"You on stilts." I can't resist a small smirk.

A growl sounds low in his throat. "Regardless of the reason why I followed you, we're in trouble."

He holds up the newspaper. My amusement disappears, replaced by cold reality.

"Randolph called me this morning."

I cross my arms over my waist. "Oh."

"Exactly." Aiden holds up the newspaper. I look away. "He was already on me about…commitment."

He spits the word out like it's poison.

"Commitment? What are you talking about?"

"Randolph's open to the New Field deal. But he had concerns about my stability."

Irritated, I look back at him. "What? You're the most stable person I know."

Something flickers across his face. "Thank you."

"You've made him millions. How can he accuse you of not being stable?"

"Because he's running for the US Senate. It's not just about money. It's about image, perception."

The crinkle of paper in his hand draws both of our gazes downward to the newspaper in his clenched hand. Slowly, he lays it on the ornate end table my mother gave me when I moved in. He stares down at the matted photo, his body so still I wonder if he's even breathing.

"It matters now."

My chest tightens. Despite everything that's happened the past twelve hours, I hate that he's facing this challenge. Yes, he may conduct his personal life in a way I don't understand. But he's one of the smartest men I know, a wizard with numbers and finances. I know what it's like to have your best qualities stripped away, to be examined under someone else's microscope and be found wanting.

"I'm sorry, Mr. Hawke."

Slowly, he turns his head to look at me. A shiver works its way down my spine at the determined glint in his eyes.

"Thank you."

He glances back down at the paper, his earlier melancholy gone. In its place is quiet determination and cold resolve.

"I did manage to pacify Randolph."

My shoulders sag in relief. Given that Brett ended up in prison, somc might find it odd that I'vc comc to carc so much about helping prisoners at a private jail. But after learning the full scope of what's going on at New Field Penitentiary, after reviewing countless testimonies and photos of the abuse that's occurred behind those walls, I've come to care about the project almost as much as Aiden.

"Good."

He looks at me then, the slight smile on his face contrasting sharply with the dark look in his eyes.

"You may not think so after I tell you what mollified him."

Warning bells clang in my head.

"What?"

"I told him we were engaged."

CHAPTER FOUR

Aiden

"ENGAGED."

Seraphina's tone is blank, her face devoid of emotion. An expression I value when she's my executive assistant. But right now, when I need an answer and need it fast, it's damned frustrating.

She's standing a few feet away, hair slipping out of a messy bun to frame her face with golden strands. A face scrubbed free of makeup, cheeks red and green eyes wide.

Beautiful.

I give myself a mental shake. That's not the direction my thoughts need to take right now.

"Yes."

Finally, she blinks. Then she swears. I've never heard her curse before.

"Why?"

I keep my gaze on her face, refrain from looking at the maroon sports bra displaying her rounded breasts, the tightness of the matching leggings clinging to her long legs.

God, this is going to be a long few months.

"Randolph has been after me to settle down, prove my longevity by committing to one woman."

I don't bother to hide my bitterness. I despise my personal life being a consideration for a client. But whether or not I like it, it's important to Randolph. And his agreement to the New Field deal is vital.

"He was concerned about the impact those photos could have on his campaign. So this solves both problems."

Seraphina rolls her eyes again. Amusement trickles in despite the gravity of the situation. I've never seen this side of her—sassy, feisty.

"How does telling him we're engaged solve anything?"

"It addresses his concerns about my ability to commit. Once we publicize our engagement, we take control of the narrative and spin it into a love story, alleviating the negative attention Randolph's concerned about."

She glares at me.

"You…but…" She puts a hand to her forehead, pushes a few strands of hair out of her face. "You're my boss."

"And I'll continue to be your boss, during and after our supposed engagement."

"No."

I still. I haven't heard *no* in a very long time. I don't like it.

"I'll double your salary."

Her mouth drops open. "What?"

"Double plus two weeks' additional vacation."

She crosses her arms over her chest, the move having the unfortunate effect of revealing the swells of her breasts more prominently.

"No."

I glance around the tiny apartment. I never pictured where Seraphina lived. Never wondered how she decorated or what kind of home she created for herself. It's jarring to think of her office at Hawke Financial, done in the same dove gray as the other offices with its gleaming mahogany desk and organized bookcases filled with binders, folders and every book on finance published in the last two years. The single family photo of her and her parents on her desk and a lone succulent plant in her window.

And I walk into this.

Oversize windows line one wall and let in streams of sunlight. Warm, sand-colored floors catch the light and glow, while a handmade rug in a dizzying kaleidoscope of bright colors lies in front of a well-worn sofa. Like someone took a rainbow, stuck it in a blender and tied the pieces together. The tiny excuse for a kitchen off to the side boasts a long marble countertop and cabinets with windows that show off the eclectic mix of dishes inside. A spiral staircase in the corner that leads up to what I guess is the lofted bed space.

I pay her over two hundred thousand dollars a year. Hers to do with as she wishes, of course, but this micro space has to be less than forty thousand a year.

"A penthouse."

Her eyes narrow. "I like my apartment."

Has she always been this stubborn? The woman could teach a class on how to stall negotiations.

I switch tactics. "Name your price."

"You're not listening to me. The answer is no." She shakes her head. "I'm not pretending to be engaged to my boss just to cater to a client."

Anger propels me forward. "I would never ask you to do that."

I stop in front of her, stare down at the woman who's been by my side for three years. A woman I thought I knew. But I don't know her. I know the persona she slips into for work, the professional mask she wears.

But the woman staring up at me… I don't know her. I've never heard her brazen retorts or seen her with fire crackling in her eyes. God knows I've never seen her body move like it did last night. The same compulsion that drew me down the path last night in pursuit of Seraphina sparks to life again. I want to know this side of Seraphina. Want to see how many layers she's hiding.

Warning bells clang in my head. But I can handle this. I've kept my desire for her under control all this time. I can maintain it while getting to know the aspects of herself she's been hiding away. A silver lining in this whole mess.

"I need him for New Field."

She stares at me for a moment longer. Then her shoulders sag.

"Oh."

I nod. "We're close, Seraphina."

"But…" Her sigh is heavy, despondent. "He's the only one who can help us, isn't he?"

Us. Despite everything that's happening, she's still a part of this, still invested.

"His media presence is growing. He's stated numerous times his views on private prisons. He has the money and the grit to conduct this takeover. And," I add grudgingly, "he's got a strong sense of morality. He won't exploit the prison for profit. He would make the changes needed, whether it's overhauling the prison or shutting it down entirely."

"You don't trust anyone. How can you trust him?"

Her words slice at me. They're true. Normally I wear my lack of trust like a badge of pride. But hearing it from someone else leaves me feeling strangely empty.

"I don't. But if I look at the factors in play, examine the odds, he's our best bet."

"And you can't buy it outright?"

She's grasping for straws. But she's wearing down. I can see it in her face, hear it in her voice.

"You know the answer to that. Hale has rejected every offer I've made. He has ties to politicians and the media and has threatened to spin a story where I'm trying to take over the prison for financial gain." Her head snaps up. "That's ridiculous!"

I can't help but smile slightly at her loyalty. I don't mention the threats he made against David, to smear my brother's name and ruin the new life he's crafted for himself. Seraphina doesn't know I have any family besides Dominic and Cassian. God willing, I'll be able to keep it that way.

"It is. But he'll do it without a second thought."

Seraphina hangs her head. "I just don't see how we can make a fake engagement work. What about my parents?"

"The fewer people who know the better. I won't even tell Cassian and Dominic the truth. Name your price," I repeat softly. Everyone has one. "Anything."

Slowly, she raises her head. Her eyes brighten.

"What about a building?"

Not the answer I was expecting. I frown. "A building? Like a penthouse or—"

"No. Grace's Refuge on West 86th Street. It's a domestic violence shelter I volunteer at. Their landlord just doubled their rent because he wants to sell the building. So," she continues, her words coming out in a torrent, "buy the building, sign it over to Grace's Refuge, and I'll be your fake fiancée."

A building. For a women's shelter. Not jewelry or clothes or a penthouse for herself. Something twists inside my chest, something unfamiliar and warm. More layers, deep ones that intrigue and touch.

My mother didn't take us to a shelter when we left Dad. We arrived in New York City in a rattletrap car with rusted floorboards and three suitcases. Mom found the cheapest apartment she could afford with the money she'd stolen out of the coffee can Dad kept on top of the refrigerator. Had we gone to a shelter, been put in touch with community programs and services that could have helped us transition, maybe she would have found a better job. Maybe things would have been different.

"Done."

Her eyes widen. "Really?"

"Yes."

She blinks several times. "Oh."

"Did you think I'd say no?"

"He's asking fifteen million."

I pull out my phone. "Landlord's name?"

"I don't know. It's a huge six-story brownstone on West 86th near Central Park West—"

I dial. Ten seconds later, a cultured male voice answers. "Good morning, Mr. Hawke."

"Good morning, Thomas. Purchase the brownstone on West 86th that currently houses Grace's Refuge. Whatever the owner's asking price is. Then coordinate with my attorneys to ensure the deed is transferred to the refuge."

"Yes, sir."

I hang up and turn back to Seraphina. She's watching me with a mixture of elation and shock.

"My part of the deal is complete."

"It is." She lets out a strangled laugh. "I shouldn't be surprised. I've watched you make seven- and eight-figure deals before your second cup of coffee. I just never..." She smiles, a deep, genuine smile that has me blinking. "Thank you."

"Don't thank me. It's business."

I inwardly curse as her smile falters, then disappears altogether. Yes, I was harsh. But I need her to know that every move I make is not rooted in anything personal. I want to get to know her better, yes, but that doesn't mean we're going to fall in love and get married and have babies together.

"Of course." She threads her fingers together and tilts her head slightly. "What do we do next, Mr. Hawke?"

I grit my teeth. "First, you need to start calling me Aiden."

She wrinkles her nose, as if she'd do anything else but utter my given name out loud.

"All right."

"Second, you'll need to move in with me."

Pink infuses her skin, starting at the base of her throat and slowly working its way up into her face. Fascinating to watch after she's kept herself contained all these years.

"Absolutely not."

"It's nonnegotiable. We need to make every effort to sell this ruse. That includes living together as an engaged couple."

"Engaged couples," she replies heatedly, "live apart all the time."

"But we won't." When she opens her mouth to retort, I hold up a hand. "It's known I don't entertain at my penthouse. Having you live there will just be more evidence that our engagement is real. And," I add with a pointed look, "I just dropped fifteen million at your request, Seraphina. Your dedication is touching, and your volunteer service will help turn public opinion in our favor, but I still held up my part of the bargain."

"How dare you." Her hands drop to her sides, her fingers curling into fists. "I volunteered because I wanted to, because…"

Her voice falters. Another secret lurking just beneath the surface.

"Because why?" I ask quietly.

"Because it's the right thing to do."

"Did you ever think of the positives that could come out of this?" I ask.

"Like what?"

"Public attention directed to Grace's Refuge. More people in need becoming aware of the services they provide and may be more likely to seek help. Increased donations." I grab the paper off the table and hold it up. "Cirque Obsidian's name is trending across the news and all social media platforms this morning. I bet if you call them, you'll find classes booked and a waiting list a mile long."

She stares at the paper. Then she turns away, the fight

disappearing as she walks over to the wall of glass. She crosses her arms and gazes out the window.

"How long?"

I swallow my triumph. I understand why she doesn't want to do this. But I'll make it worth her while, from buying the building for the shelter to upping her salary and vacation.

"March. Ten months."

She flinches. Most women I've dated would have jumped at a chance like this.

"That will give Randolph and me enough time to make sure the takeover goes through. I don't want to end things until Hale is out."

"And I'm to live with you? The whole time?"

I never invite women to my penthouse. Or really anyone except Dominic and Cassian, and even that is rare. It's my space, my sanctuary. But the thought of Seraphina in my home, of waking up to her presence every morning for nearly a year, makes the craving I've been suppressing grow until it gnaws at me, an unsatiated hunger I want to fill.

I'll have to keep my hands off her. She's still my employee, and will continue to work for me after this whole mess is over. But I'm going to thoroughly enjoy exploring the woman I've caught glimpses of in the past twelve hours.

"Yes."

She drops her head back, stares up at the ceiling. Then, slowly, she turns around. Her face is blank except for her eyes. That green, so vivid just minutes ago, is dull now.

"What about other women?"

"No."

I snap the word out with the ferocity of cracking a whip. Twenty years and I can still feel the pain, white-hot and sharp, when I realized the girl I thought I loved hadn't just cheated on me but had left me behind to take the blame for a crime I didn't commit.

"This engagement will be in name only, but I will give it the same focus I do any other relationship. I expect the same."

She shrugs, as if she couldn't care less whether or not I continued to carry out discreet affairs. I, on the other hand, can easily picture punching any other man who even dares to think about taking her on a date, let alone kissing her.

"I don't date much."

How selfish a bastard am I that her words send relief rushing through me? Since I've hired Seraphina, I've dated ten women. Ten women whose company I enjoyed, both in and out of bed. But not a single one tempted me the way Seraphina does.

Because she's untouchable.

I grasp that thought and hold on to it with both hands. If we were to sleep together, which we won't, my fascination would go away.

"Mutual fidelity. Ten months, with our engagement terminated at the end of March of next year. You'll reside within my penthouse and continue to work for Hawke Financial. We'll go out regularly—restaurants, museums, galas. See and be seen as much as possible. Occasional displays of affection when in public." She blanches. "Just in public, Seraphina. You'll have your own room at the penthouse. And," I add softly, "if there's something you think of, something you want, I will give it to you if I can."

"There won't be anything." She lets out a long, shuddering breath. "All right."

I cross to her, not caring for the sudden tension that grips her as I draw near.

"Thank you."

She meets my gaze head-on, some of the fire from before flickering in the green depths. "If New Field wasn't a part of this, I wouldn't agree."

"If New Field wasn't a part of this, I wouldn't be asking."

Her brows draw together. "I've never understood why it's so important to you." Before I can think of an answer, she looks away. "But it's none of my business."

One of the things that I've always appreciated about her is her adherence to protocol, her dedication to professionalism. Strangely enough, though, part of me wants to share. I told her I learned of New Field's abuse through a trusted confidant. She doesn't know David, my biological brother, exists, let alone that he stole a car, crossed state lines during the pursuit, and crashed into a semitruck. A horrible choice, and one he had to pay the price for.

Just not the price Hale and his demons exacted when David was sent to New Field Penitentiary. The fact that David even survived his time in isolation is a miracle.

"What do we do next?"

I refocus on Seraphina and can't help but smirk. "Your executive assistant persona is showing."

She arches a brow. "I do best when I have a plan."

"As do I." My eyes roam over her apartment. "How quickly can you pack?"

"Pack? You mean move in today?"

"Yes. The press are swarming and…" My voice trails off as my phone buzzes. I read the text and smile. "We'll need to do some shopping. Clothes, shoes, an engagement ring. We have a photo shoot tomorrow morning at nine."

"Photo shoot?"

Her voice pitches up as her arms tighten over her chest, pushing her incredible breasts even higher.

"Dylan Greene with *Gilded Magazine.* She's agreed to come to the penthouse tomorrow for a photo shoot and interview that will be featured in next month's editorial."

"And when," Seraphina hisses, "did you make that call?"

"On my way here."

"What if I'd said no?"

"You didn't."

If looks could kill, I'd be lying dead on her rainbow rug.

My smile disappears. "I may not know the Seraphina who dances with fire or the one who lives in a teeny apartment," I say as I walk closer, "but I do know Seraphina the executive assistant. I've seen how much you've poured into this. I know how much it means to you. There's no way you'd let it fall apart."

Her mouth tightens. "I'll start packing. But I think, Mr. Hawke—"

"Aiden."

"I think, *Aiden*, you're the most calculating person I've ever met."

She turns before I can retort, and heads for the staircase. Her movements are quick, graceful. Movements I recognized last night before I finally accepted who the fire dancer was.

She disappears from view. Moments later I hear drawers being pulled out then slammed back into place, the faint rustle of fabric, the loud zipper of a suitcase.

Not the best start to our engagement. But I know Seraphina will hold up her end of our deal. She'll see this through to the end. And then we can go back to how things were. Boss and secretary, a team.

And nothing more.

CHAPTER FIVE

Seraphina

THE LIMO PULLS up in front of a store I know very well even though I've never been inside. There are several stunning dresses in the window, including a black satin evening gown with a halter neckline and daring cutout in the center of the chest covered only by dark lace.

The kind of dress I would never wear in a million years. But exactly the kind of dress one of Aiden's previous girlfriends would have worn. Unwelcome jealousy curls through me. I tamp it down lest the man seated across from me looks up from his phone and notices an expression I don't feel like explaining.

I glance at him out of the corner of my eye. His hair is brushed to one side, his jaw set as he types something out. We've barely said two words to each other since he rushed me into the limo.

After he walked into my apartment and upended my life, I took thirty minutes to pack a couple of suitcases and a backpack. Aiden offered to send movers for the rest, but a quick glare cut him off.

I love my apartment. The night I finally left Brett, I

fled with the clothes on my back and my wallet. I didn't even risk grabbing my phone off the charger. I ended up at Grace's Refuge for three days before I finally got the courage to call my parents and tell them what had happened, that they had been right and I'd been in an abusive relationship for years. What made it worse was how kind they were. They offered for me to move back in with them, but I didn't want to leave New York, didn't want Brett to chase me out of the city I loved. And I definitely didn't want to accept anything from my parents, even though they offered to pay the first month's rent on a new place. One of the client advocates at Grace's Refuge found my studio apartment a week later. It's been home for the last three years and I'm not giving it up. I need my place, a tether to the life I'm leaving behind, the one I'll return to in ten months when this ridiculous charade is over.

"Ready?"

I start and turn just as Aiden leans over and opens the door. My breath hitches and I lean back. He gives me a curious glance as he climbs out and then extends a hand. I hesitate. Then, slowly, I place my hand in his.

His fingers curl around mine as he gently guides me out of the limo, his bare palm resting against mine. Did he see the slight tremor when his fingers closed over mine? I look at the store, the sidewalk, anything but him. This man has already seen far more of me than I'd like him to. I don't need him to see just how deep my attraction to him runs.

My phone rings as the chauffeur closes the door behind us. I pull it out of my pocket and grimace. Jessica. She's called no less than a dozen times in the last hour. I hit the I'll call you back later automatic text reply and slide the phone back into my pocket. I called my parents while I was packing, a call that went as well as I'd expected. Which is to say, horribly. I don't blame them. Here they thought I was still trying to get up the courage to start dating again, only to find out their daughter has supposedly been dating her boss for months and just got engaged.

I don't know which was worse—my mother's teary voice or my father's threats to kidnap Aiden and drop him off at some random truck stop in the middle of nowhere if he hurt me.

I'll need to talk to Jessica soon. But I need a break.

"Everything all right?"

I can't help it. I laugh. "No, Mr. Hawke, everything is not all right."

He doesn't correct me on his name. Instead, he faces me and takes my other hand in his so both are held captive in his grasp.

"I know things are progressing rapidly—"

"I just lied to my parents." God, I would love nothing more than a good cry and a steaming caramel latte right now. "I had to tell them all sorts of lies and you know what? They're worried about me."

God, I can't believe I'm putting them through this again. They spent three of the four years I was with Brett worrying about me. Toward the end, they were terrified.

And now they're scared again. Because of me.

"If there had been another way, I would have made it happen."

I tug my hands out of his grasp. "I know. I know being engaged is the last thing you ever wanted."

He doesn't answer, just watches me with fathomless eyes.

"Let's go," I finally murmur.

We walk up to the doors. The interior is dark, with the hours clearly written on the glass, including Closed Sunday.

"Looks like we'll need to come back."

The words are barely out of my mouth when the lights flicker on and a tall woman with thick black curls walks into view. She grins at both of us with an enthusiasm I'm not prepared to deal with after my life's been upended. But I force myself to give her a tiny smile and wave back as she opens the door.

"Good morning, come in!"

She opens the door and ushers us in. A cool blast of air greets us, as does the sight of dozens of stunning dresses hanging from silver bars, handbags displayed in recessed shelves with bright lights accentuating every expensive detail, and mannequins draped in beautiful jackets. Why on earth did I just throw a T-shirt on over my sports bra?

"I'm Brenda, your stylist." She inclines her head to Aiden. "We're so excited to serve you and your fiancée today, Mr. Hawke."

Another forced smile as Brenda looks at me. I probably look the opposite of a happily engaged woman.

"Thank you." I watch the charm come out as Aiden shakes Brenda's hand. He smiles, still one that doesn't reach his eyes, but most wouldn't know it's a fake smile unless they knew him well. "As I mentioned to your manager earlier this morning, we're on a special shopping expedition to buy some new outfits for Seraphina. Our engagement recently became public and we're looking forward to going out more."

"Oh!" Dimples appear in Brenda's cheeks as she grins. "I'm both honored and excited to serve you today." She turns to me. "What are your preferences? Do you have a list?"

I glance over at Aiden, but he gestures for me to answer. A knot loosens in my chest. The last year of Brett's and my relationship was a balancing act when it came to what I wore. I tried dressing in outfits that met his standards. But so often I fell short. I'm glad to see that Aiden's need for control doesn't extend to my clothes, because our engagement would be over as quickly as it's begun.

"Um… I'm not sure," I confess. What does a billionaire's fiancée wear?

"Cocktail dresses," Aiden says with that smile still in place. "Evening gowns, a few outfits for media appearances, and resort wear."

I try not to sound ungrateful as I look over at him. "Do I really need all of that?"

"Of course you do. Darling," he adds with what sounds suspiciously like amusement. He turns back to Brenda. "She usually likes vintage-inspired pieces."

A fluttering sensation flies through my chest. Yet another detail Aiden paid attention to.

It doesn't mean anything, I remind myself firmly.

"We have some beautiful dresses I know you'll like." Brenda clasps her hands in front of her. "What sort of budget are we aiming for?"

"There isn't one." Aiden gestures to the store. "Clothing, jewelry, handbags. Whatever she needs, whatever she wants."

My head starts to spin. No limit? In a store like this? After he just dropped fifteen million dollars to buy a town house for a charity he's never heard of?

I wait until Brenda disappears into the back before I turn to him.

"Is all of this really necessary?"

"Yes. We'll be under constant scrutiny from here on out. I need you to look the part of a billionaire's fiancée."

I think of the numerous women he's been seen with since I started working with Hawke Financial. They wear clothes like this on a daily basis.

"It's nothing to do with your style, Seraphina."

I wrinkle my nose. Is the man reading my mind?

"I didn't say—"

"No, but the stricken look on your face spoke volumes." He moves closer, so close I have to tilt my head to look up at him. "If I had concerns about your clothing, I'd have brought it up a long time ago. You have always represented Hawke Financial well, both professionally and fashionably."

Damn it, why does that compliment warm me so much? I know how much Hawke Financial means to him, the hours he's poured into making it successful.

"Maybe you'll even enjoy yourself."

"I'm not exactly a marathon shopping kind of girl." Much to my mother's chagrin.

"Well, do your best, then." He glances down at his watch. "I should be back in two hours."

"Two hours?" Spending time with Aiden isn't high on my radar right now, but it's preferable to being left here alone. "Where are you going?"

"I have a couple errands to run. I'll be back by eleven." He nods to Brenda as she comes back into the room with several gowns draped over her arm. "Take good care of her."

And then he's gone, walking out the door without a backward glance, leaving me alone in the middle of one of the most high-end fashion stores in the city. I watch as he gets back into the limo and the long, sleek car pulls away from the curb.

"Ready, Miss Clark?"

I turn back to Brenda.

"Uh…yeah." I shake my head. "Sorry, it's been a hectic morning."

"I can only imagine." Brenda smiles, her red lipstick bright against her dark skin. "Don't let the media bother you. We get plenty of celebrities in here on what they think is the worst day of their lives, but things always turn around."

Some of my tension bleeds out. "Thank you, Brenda."

"You're welcome." She holds up the dresses. "Let's see if we can make it better."

Aiden

I press the buzzer for the boutique at five minutes 'til eleven. The box in my jacket pocket thumps gently against my thigh.

The last two hours were a rush of phone calls to Dominic and Cassian to speaking at length with my human resources and public relations consultants to ensure Seraphina and I stay within legalities while presenting the best possible front.

I also called George Randolph again. He didn't sound like he was about to spit bullets, but he was still gruff and short. He declined my offer to have dinner with Seraphina and me this week. But he is coming to the Violet Masquerade next weekend. And he's agreed to meet with Seraphina and me the day before to discuss not only our engagement but the New Field deal.

The clock's ticking. A week to convince the world that Seraphina and I are desperately in love and create a positive narrative that will convince Randolph to continue to do business with me.

I think of David. Of Mom. I will not fail.

The lock disengages and I walk in. Brenda comes down the white marble staircase at the far end of the store.

"Hello, Mr. Hawke!"

"Hello again, Brenda." I glance at the stairs. "How's Seraphina doing?"

"Wonderful," Brenda beams. "She's picked out some lovely pieces. Needed a little encouragement, but I think we got her set up with everything she needed."

"Thank you."

"You're welcome." She hesitates. "Forgive me if this is too forward, but she's very kind. You're a lucky man."

I smile slightly. "I am."

Brenda nods toward the stairs. "She's trying on one last gown. I'll be up in a few minutes with boxes for her purchases."

I pass by a grand piano and ascend the circular stairs. The jewelry box gently taps against my thigh with every step. When I walked into the store next door, I had a plan: buy the most expensive ring. I don't know how to share my feelings, nor do I care to learn. But I do know how to treat the women in my life well, showering them with gifts in lieu of emotional fondness. To date, only a couple have pushed for more in terms of affection.

But as the owner pulled out some of his priciest rings, one caught my eye. As soon as I took a better look, I knew it was the one for Seraphina. The engagement might be fake, but her loyalty is real, as is her commitment to seeing the New Field deal through. She deserves a ring that's more her style.

The last time I bought something for a woman because I thought she'd like it was Melanie. A silver necklace with a crescent moon after weeks of saving change from the wallets we stole. When I presented it to her, she'd told me she liked it even as she played with the diamond studs in her ears.

Idiot. The signs were there almost from the beginning. She used me, and I was too lovesick, too desperate for an emotional attachment, that I let myself be blinded.

Never again. I've kept that vow for the past twenty years. I won't break it for anyone. But that doesn't mean I can't do something nice for Seraphina, especially after seeing how much her parents' reaction to the news of our engagement hurt her.

I near the top of the stairs. A not insignificant slice of guilt powered my decision-making. I hadn't thought about the impact our engagement would have on Seraphina's loved ones. I've seen the photo of her and her parents on her desk, know that she visits them at least twice a month. I'd lay my life on the line for Dominic and Cassian, but I don't share personal details with them. Even David and I keep our private lives private despite getting together once a month.

But it hurt her. Hurt the people she loves. The stricken

look on her face when I asked if everything was all right, followed by that empty laugh I've never heard from her before, cut me.

This is just one of many reasons I'm not meant for a long-term relationship. I become fixated on projects, on goals and deadlines, to the point of not seeing anything or anyone else. It's a hard habit to break, especially when it's led to so much success.

I reach the top of the stairs. Another long hallway with alcoves leading into private dressing rooms, complete with antique-inspired lounge furniture, small chandeliers, and silk curtains hiding the changing room behind the gilded mirrors.

I glance to my right. And freeze.

Seraphina is standing on a dais in front of a mirror. She's facing away from me, her hair still pulled up into the same loose bun, leaving her back bare to my gaze.

My cock grows so hard it's almost painful. My eyes roam over the line of black satin that starts just above her waist and falls into sweeping folds about her feet. As my gaze travels up, I note the satin looped around her neck.

From my vantage point, I can see part of Seraphina's face in the mirror and a hint of the satin crossing over one breast. She's staring at her reflection as if she's never seen herself like this. There's a hint of wonder, a shy smile as she turns this way and that.

The ache in my chest grows, a desire to peel back the layers of Seraphina Clark and find out…everything. It may not be as satisfying as sex, but if it's the only thing I can have without crossing the line, I'll take it.

"Stunning."

She immediately stiffens. Our eyes meet in the mirror before she turns around.

"How long have you been standing there?"

I would answer, but I can't, not with my tongue in my throat after I just swallowed it. The satin swaths crisscross just below her neck and cover her breasts. But then there's nothing except black lace in the middle. Lace woven thin enough I can see the swells of her breasts.

"Long enough."

I drag my gaze back up to her face. The wariness on her face doesn't fully hide her awareness of me. The faint glossing of her eyes, another blush creeping up her neck as her breathing quickens.

I enjoy every single second as I walk closer.

"It's just missing one thing."

She frowns and glances down. "What?"

I pull the box out of my pocket and hold it out. "This."

I close the last steps between us and hold it up. She watches every move I make. Her eyes are the only thing moving as she watches me open the box.

Her gasp makes me smile.

"Oh my God." She stares at the ring before wrenching her gaze up. "Mr. Hawke—"

"Aiden."

She wrinkles her nose. "*Aiden*, I can't accept that."

Irritation creeps in. "Would it help if I told you it wasn't the most expensive ring in the store?"

There. The tiniest quirk of her lips.

"Perhaps. Still, it's..."

"It's what?"

She arches one brow with that never-before-seen sass I'm coming to enjoy so much.

"It was more than a thousand dollars."

"True. But it reminded me of your eyes."

Damn. I didn't mean to let that slip. But as her eyes soften and she looks at me with warmth instead of the distaste she did earlier this morning, I don't regret it.

I pull the ring out of the box and grasp her hand, relish her sharp inhale. Almost as much as I enjoy the feel of her hand in mine. It's been three years since I held her hand when we shook hands at the end of her interview. There's been the occasional brush of fingers when she handed over a report, shoulders nudging when we stood in an elevator or crowded conference room.

But holding her hand like this isn't just sexy as hell. The intimacy of our palms stressed together sends a shockwave through me.

I slide the ring on her finger. The sight of that emerald winking up at me from her hand, a ring I picked out to mark her as mine to the world, deepens my craving for her. She's not mine. Never will be. But I'm going to thoroughly enjoy pretending she is for the next ten months.

Seraphina holds her hand up and takes a closer look at the ring.

"It's breathtaking. Thank you."

The gratitude in her eyes hits me square in the chest. I can't recall a single woman I've dated look at me with such simple appreciation. But the women I've dated have all been from the world I've spent nearly twenty years in. They're used to lavish jewelry and high-end fashion.

And this is why I'm so selective. So that emotions like the ones I'm witnessing play across Seraphina's face don't come into play.

"You're welcome."

Her smile dims a little at the abrupt change in my tone. She glances down at the ring again, then turns back to the mirror. I grit my teeth at the sight of her back. It's all too easy to imagine trailing my fingers down the smooth skin, followed by my lips as I slowly undress her.

"Did Brenda say when she was coming back up?"

"No, she mentioned grabbing boxes for your purchases. Why?"

Seraphina huffs. "The zipper is stuck. I'm afraid if I tug too much, I'll rip the fabric."

I should go get Brenda. Have her help. Keep my distance from Seraphina like I just told myself I would.

Instead, I walk toward the dais. Watch as her chest rises and falls, her eyes fixed on mine in the mirror.

"May I?"

Slowly, she nods. Points to the zipper just above the small of her back. I grab the dress with one hand and tug. The zipper doesn't budge. But my knuckles graze her skin. Possessiveness strikes, sinks its fangs into my chest, the initial bite followed by a burn as I glimpse blue lace beneath the satin.

Slowly, I raise my head. Seraphina is watching me, eyes glittering with an answering desire that has my finger tightening on the back of her dress. She leans back slightly, as if giving me permission to pull her off the dais into my arms.

I knew she wanted me last night by the lakeshore. But to see it in the light of day makes me want to keep unzipping, peel the dress off before turning her around and kissing her senseless. Finally taste her lips, run my hands over her incredible body.

I let go of the zipper and step back. Regain some composure before I speak.

"I'll be downstairs when you're ready."

I don't wait to see her reaction. I need distance. I don't mix business with pleasure. But after just a brief time in Seraphina's company this morning, I can barely keep my eyes or hands off her.

I won't cross the line of having sex with my assistant, won't risk introducing a dynamic that could potentially devastate our working relationship. She is far too valuable, knows my quirks and preferences, knows my clients.

And damn it, I like her. I don't like many people, but I like Seraphina, respect her. Which means I just need to leave her untouched during this charade.

No matter how much both of us seem to want otherwise.

CHAPTER SIX

Seraphina

I STARE AT my reflection in the mirror. It's me, but it doesn't look like me. My hair is twisted up into an elegant arrangement of curls. I'm wearing a stunning ivory dress with cap sleeves, full skirt and a row of pearl buttons up the back. It's the most expensive dress I've ever owned. Half my month's salary. Surprisingly, I like it. As I do a small twirl in front of the mirror and watch the skirt flare out, I have to admit, Brenda has excellent taste. I love the vintage vibe, the subtle elegance. It makes me feel a little more ready for the *Gilded* photo shoot.

A little. Maybe like a teeny-tiny fraction more ready. Whether it meets with Aiden's vision for his fiancée is another matter entirely.

Doubt creeps into my chest. The movie starlet he dated last fall favored name-brand couture with elaborate details like feathers and intricate beading, even a dramatic fifteen-foot train at one of her movie premieres. Not a vintage-inspired dress that would be more suited for a quiet garden wedding.

The premiere, I remember, that Aiden refused to attend. A week before Thanksgiving. The actress had cut things off via a phone call I'd patched through, wincing as I'd forwarded it to Aiden's primary line. She'd been furious, rattling off a string of creative curses as soon as I answered.

I'd sent her flowers, like I do to all of Aiden's exes. She'd sent them back in a long black box reminiscent of a coffin, stems broken and petals shredded. Aiden had merely raised his eyebrows when he'd opened the lid and beheld the floral destruction.

"Better the flowers than me."

The man is cold. Ice-cold. Yet there was nothing but heat in his eyes as he unzipped my dress at the store yesterday. When our gazes met in the mirror, I saw his desire, saw the same need in him that was pulsing through me like lava. And when his fingers grazed my bare back, I had to clench my thighs together at the sudden sensation flooding my core. I had a sudden, vivid image of undoing his belt and filling my hands with him. Sinking down onto my knees and taking him in my mouth, bringing him to the edge of control.

The wickedness of my fantasy left me flushed and excited. I chastised myself for even thinking of my boss that way. But a small part of me was grateful. It's been so long since I've slept with a man I half wondered if a part of me was irrevocably broken, that I would never be intimately attracted to a man again.

When I walked out fifteen minutes later, the old Aiden was back. Calm, collected. The limo took us to Central Park South, one of the skyscrapers along Billionaires Row, and past a crowd of photographers outside. Photographers, I realized with shock, that were there to catch a glimpse of us. Of *me.* It made me want to ask the chauffeur to take me back to my apartment so I could lock the doors, draw the blinds and pretend like none of this was happening.

Thankfully the ride up to Aiden's penthouse in the ultrafast elevator distracted me. Forty-one seconds, he informed me when I stepped out of the elevator and into the most glamorous, expensive penthouse I'd ever seen. Stone walls offset by the occasional black accent wall. Huge windows that overlooked Central Park. The terrace, featuring a saltwater pool, sunken firepit, and its own gazebo at the far end. A massive kitchen with obsidian counters that looked so pristine I wondered if they had ever been used.

And my bedroom. It's like walking into a dream, from the massive bed with its teal-colored velvet headboard to my own balcony with a soaking tub.

Throughout the tour, Aiden acted more like a tour guide than the man who had looked ready to devour me in the dressing room. I was confused, then embarrassed as we walked through the penthouse. Had I imagined the whole thing?

After the tour, he excused himself and disappeared into his office. I didn't see him until dinner, a delicious meal catered from an exclusive Italian restaurant in Greenwich Village. The lobster ravioli tasted like ash in my mouth as we went over our story again and again. It was almost eight o'clock when he excused himself for a conference call and I tumbled into bed.

I haven't seen him since. But in less than ten minutes, we'll be pretending to be an engaged couple in love instead of boss and executive assistant.

What could go wrong?

The thought of posing with Aiden, selling a lie in front of cameras that will document our every move, makes me want to crawl beneath the down comforter on my massive bed and sleep the rest of the day away.

I glance down at the ring on my left hand. The emerald winks up at me from its resting place inside a circle of tiny diamonds shaped like teardrops. When Aiden slipped the ring onto my finger, I wished it was real. Stupid, of course. But it's the first time a man has ever given me a ring. And then there were his words, so sweet and unexpected I stood there and blinked at him like an owl.

"It reminded me of your eyes."

The same line, I remind myself firmly, he's probably used with countless other women.

The ding of the elevator echoes up the stairs and down the hall. I smooth my hands over the skirt one last time. Straighten my shoulders and do one last check of my makeup.

"Showtime," I whisper.

I walk out of my room with the enthusiasm of a prisoner walking to their sentencing. But I remind myself as I walk down the long hall with its one wall fashioned of glass that overlooks the city, it could be worse. Much worse.

It's not even been forty-eight hours, but there's been no whisper of Brett's name or my past relationship. For the dozenth time since this whole mess started, I murmur a quiet prayer of thanks that I listened to my dad and petitioned the court to identify me only by my initials in the records pertaining to my case. One of the few positives about cutting myself off from almost everyone those last two years Brett and I dated was that almost no one from college or work knew the extent of the abuse.

Maybe, just maybe, I'll get through this with the most humiliating and degrading time of my life staying buried in the past.

I descend the stairs, my fingers wrapped around the railing in a death grip. The wall disappears, revealing the stunning two-story living room with its floor-to-ceiling windows. The dark wood-planked ceiling, the low-slung leather furniture done in shades of chestnut, the recessed lighting, all of it screams that a very wealthy man lives here.

A man who is currently standing at the doors leading out to the terrace, shoulders thrown back, one hand on his hip and the other pressing his phone to his ear.

I pause. Even in his own home, Aiden Hawke exudes confidence, control.

And a complete inability to relax.

The low rumble of his voice brushes over my skin like a silky caress, one that heightens my awareness and draws my attention to the dark wisps of hair grazing his collar. If this were a real engagement, I'd walk up behind him, run my fingers through his hair, give his sculpted rear a playful tap. Just because he's not the right man for me doesn't mean I can't notice his near-perfect physique.

But he's not the right man for me. This isn't a real relationship. Despite what happened with Brett, I maintain hope I can have a family of my own one day. A husband who loves and respects me, children I can spoil rotten. I've seen plenty of examples of happy couples, including my own parents. I need to get out of my own head and start dating again. Every time I've tried I've panicked, backpedaled.

I need to keep my focus on fulfilling the terms of our arrangement and off Aiden in any personal sense, including lust. As he stated, both when he first proposed this idea and when he presented me with a formal contract to sign last night, the engagement is in name only. No sex, no physical touching unless necessary for the sake of the ruse.

With a silent warning to my hormones, I move down the last remaining stairs in time to hear Aiden say, "Believe it, Cass."

There's a pause, followed by Aiden's quiet chuckle. A genuine laugh that sinks into me and settles low in my belly. I've never heard him laugh like that.

"Don't worry about flying back. We'll be in Venice on Friday for the masquerade."

Venice? A thrill shoots through me. He's talking about the annual charity gala he's hosted every summer for the past few years. An event sponsored by the Hawke Foundation, a charity put together by the Hawke men with proceeds split between four charities, one for each brother and one in honor of their late adoptive father. They've all invested a significant amount into the foundation, but they also each host their own fundraiser every year, stunning events designed to draw the wealthiest donors and raise awareness of the charities they support.

Including the Violet Masquerade, an opulent affair hosted in the Palazzo Pisani Moretta along the Grand Canal. A literal palace with stunning stone staircases, a grand hall with a frescoed ceiling and jaw-dropping chandeliers that's draped with flowers and filled with music every summer.

Not that I would know. Everything I know about the Violet Masquerade has come from the pictures posted on social media from the lucky guests invited to attend. Aiden's offered to fly me out every year since I started working for him. But I've said no every time, always telling myself it wouldn't be appropriate, that people might gossip.

Truthfully, though, I didn't want to see him dancing with one of his girlfriends, wonder what they were doing when they slipped away from the crowds.

"Enough."

I stiffen at the abrupt change in Aiden's voice. No trace of warmth or brotherly affection now. Just frozen steel.

"I appreciate the concern, Cassian, but I don't require any assistance. Go meet your new client and we'll talk next week."

He hangs up and turns around so quickly I don't have time to pretend like I wasn't eavesdropping. Aiden stares at me, displeasure clearly written across his long, handsome face.

"I'm sorry." I hold his gaze even though I want to sink into the floor. "I should have let you know I was here."

He's frowning at me now, his gaze sweeping down to my nude heels and back up to my new pearl earrings.

I glance down at my dress. "What?"

"You look…" His frown deepens. "Fine."

Ouch.

"Thank you, Mr. Hawke."

I use my most professional executive secretary voice. Aiden's eyes narrow.

"You're mocking me."

"I wouldn't dare, sir. Although," I add sweetly, "given that you just subtly insulted my appearance, I think I'm entitled to at least one mocking statement."

He moves, his stride sure as his long legs eat up the distance between us in mere seconds. I can't help the sudden fluttering of my pulse, the heat spearing through me straight to my core. What is missing as he stops just a couple feet away is fear.

The realization startles me. I'm alone with a man literally a quarter of a mile above the city. The first time I've been alone with a man in his home in years. But I know with complete certainty Aiden would never lay a hand on me in anger.

Relief weakens my knees. If I can trust Aiden, maybe there is hope for me yet. Maybe this fake engagement will give me a chance to practice, to get comfortable around a man and start dating again once our arrangement ends.

Aiden slides his hands into his pockets as he regards me. The frown is gone, replaced by a curiosity that makes me want to squirm.

"How many times," he finally asks, "have I not seen you?"

I blink. "What?"

He steps closer. My throat narrows to the point I almost gasp for air. He slides one hand out of his pocket and reaches up. I tense. The frown returns as his hand drops back to his side.

"Keep in mind we have to convince the world we've been secretly dating for six months."

"Since the office New Year's party." I nod. "I've memorized everything."

"Memorization won't matter if we can't sell the ruse."

"Well, it's a little hard to fake intimacy with your boss."

A small lie. Yes, it's odd holding Aiden's hand and hearing him call me "darling." But I also like it, like it far too much to let my guard down and just throw myself into the role.

My phone dings. I pull it out of the pocket of my dress, shame creeping in as I read my mother's message.

Good luck this morning. Your father and I hope it goes well!

"What is it?"

I sigh as I type back a reply. "My mom. Just wishing us good luck."

He waits until I slide my phone back into my pocket. "How did they respond?"

"They were concerned."

I can't blame my parents for their anger and fear. Waking up to find out your daughter who went through a traumatic relationship is now engaged to the boss she's been supposedly secretly dating for six months? Yeah, I'd be panicked and pissed off, too.

"But your mom feels better about it now?"

I shrug. After our brief morning conversation, I spent an hour on the phone with both of them that afternoon, then another forty minutes with my mom just before Aiden came back to the penthouse. Long, long conversations reassuring them I wasn't being kidnapped or blackmailed, that I truly loved Aiden and he loved me.

How I got those words out without laughing or breaking down, I'll never know.

"I think she's just trying to be kind. Make sure she doesn't push me away."

The bell for the elevator rings, signaling someone at the bottom is requesting permission to come up. Aiden walks over to the screen next to the elevator doors and taps the monitor.

"The team from *Gilded* is here."

Oh God. Thoughts of my parents fade away as my own panic surfaces. Can I do this? Can I actually pretend to be in love with Aiden Hawke?

"You twirled a stick around your neck while the stick was on fire."

"And?" I ask as I try to get a grip on myself. "I'm the one in control when I dance."

He pushes buttons on the monitor. A ding sounds, signaling the elevator has started its ascent.

"Forty-one seconds."

He crosses the room and cups my face in his hands. Before I can even draw a breath, his lips are on mine.

CHAPTER SEVEN

Seraphina

AIDEN HAWKE IS kissing me.

I stand there, frozen, acutely aware of…everything. His scent, the heat of his palms against my face, the press of his mouth against mine. Sensation spirals up, like hundreds of butterflies being released and filling my chest with an incredible fluttering even as my heart pounds against my ribs.

So I slide my hands up his chest and kiss him back. I part my lips, inviting him in.

He tenses. Oh no. Did I make a mistake?

I start to pull back. But Aiden slides a hand around the back of my neck as he groans.

And then he's kissing me again. No, he's devouring me, his tongue sliding along the seam of my lips before slipping inside. The intimacy of it sends a shudder through my body all the way down to my thighs. I press my legs together as a terribly delicious ache starts to pulse deep inside me. I fist my fingers in his shirt and hold on so I don't collapse in a puddle at his feet.

When I entertained the occasional daydream about

Aiden, I always stopped before I let my own musings go too far. Not only did it feel wrong to think about my boss like that, but being intimate with a man wasn't something I was ready for.

But I'm ready now.

I press myself against Aiden, moan as one hand comes up my side and stops just below my breast. I've never felt like this, electrified from one single kiss that's both torture and heaven.

He leans back, gazing down at me with hooded eyes and mouth stained with my lipstick.

"Aiden," I murmur, leaning up for another kiss.

He smiles at me, the first real smile he's ever given me. It transforms his entire face, softening the harsh planes of his cheekbones and the bluntness of his jaw as his eyes crinkle at the corners. A different warmth blooms in my chest, rooted in desire but fed by deeper emotion.

"Much better," he murmurs.

It's like being splashed with ice water. Humiliation replaces my brief moment of affection. Aiden might have enjoyed the kiss, but he didn't do it because he wanted to. He did it to relax me, to make me feel more comfortable with his touch before the photographers arrive.

I step back. "At least something meets your approval."

Aiden's brows draw together. His lips part, but before he can say anything, the elevator chimes three times just before the doors open.

Showtime.

One of the most sophisticated-looking women I've ever seen steps out of the elevator. Black hair sliced off just below her jaw accentuates the angularness of her face.

Dressed in long black trousers and shirt with a white blazer, the woman strides up to Aiden, hand outstretched.

"Mr. Hawke. I'm Dylan Greene."

Aiden shakes her hand. "Thank you for coming, Ms. Greene."

"Thank you for inviting me." Her smile is quick, sharp. "We're thrilled you selected *Gilded* to announce your engagement." She gestures to the young man behind her dressed in similar black pants and a shirt. "My photographer, Liam." Her gaze slides to me. "And you must be Seraphina Clark."

The way she eyes me makes me think of sharks and lions, predators on the hunt.

Just like a tough client.

I move forward, offering my hand as I slip into a professional mindset. If I treat this interview like I would any other client meeting, I can maintain the calm I need. I just need to balance that with holding Aiden's hand and occasionally kissing his cheek.

No pressure whatsoever.

"Hello, Ms. Greene." I smile, give her a firmer handshake than I normally would have. "I want to echo Aiden's sentiments and thank you for coming."

Dylan's smile grows. "But of course. The world is dying to know more about you."

Exactly what I don't want. I turn to see Aiden standing next to me. Might as well start the charade now. I slide my hand into his, biting back a smile when his body tenses next to me.

Good. Let him feel uncomfortable for a minute or two.

"I also appreciate you understanding if I'm nervous." I glance up at Aiden, giving him the most adoring gaze I can. "We've been keeping our relationship under the radar for so long it's odd talking about it in public."

"Of course," Dylan croons.

Aiden squeezes my hand. I glance at him and release the breath I hadn't even realized I'd been holding when I see the admiration in his eyes. I'm still hurt by how he used our kiss, confused by his transition from flirty fake fiancé to cold, distant billionaire. But I'll take whatever support I can get right now.

A camera clicks. I start and look back at the photographer.

"Sorry," he says with a smile that says he's not sorry at all. "Great candid moment."

"A warning, next time," Aiden replies. His voice is quiet, but the menace in his tone is crystal clear. Liam shrinks back a fraction.

"Of course, sir. My apologies."

"Let's start on the terrace," Dylan interjects with another megawatt smile. "Before the sun gets too high. We'll take the photos, and then we'll sit down and chat."

As soon as we get outside, she directs us to a navy chaise longue. She starts off with a simple pose of me sitting and Aiden standing behind me, his hand on my shoulder. Liam sets up his camera as Dylan watches us with a critical eye.

Click, click.

Aiden's hand tightens slightly on my shoulder. I reach up without thinking and cover his hand with my own.

"Oh, perfect!" Dylan points to my hand. "Liam, close-up of the ring."

A few more shots and then she instructs me to sit on

one side of the chaise and Aiden to sit on the other. We face each other, a few inches between us.

"Okay, Mr. Hawke, if you could lean in closer, maybe put a hand to her face."

I try not to tense as he reaches up. Try to act like he's done this every day for the past six months. But when his hand settles on my face, cradling my jaw with a tenderness I know is just for the cameras, I can't help but lean into his touch.

There. Something flares in his eyes as the camera starts clicking away, a glimpse of the same fire I saw yesterday in the mirror before he turned and left me partially undressed.

"Foreheads together," Dylan instructs.

Slowly, I lean forward. Aiden's nostrils flare as his eyes darken. My glance drops to his lips. I hate that a fake kiss was the best one of my life. Hate that I can remember every second: the pressure of his hands on my face, the possessive press of his mouth on mine. That moment when he seemed to come undone and deepened the kiss until I had to cling to him to stay standing.

Our foreheads touch and my lips part on a sigh. Even though this is just for a show, I feel that connection that pulsed between us at the gala reignite, strengthen.

If him just touching my face and laying his head against mine makes me feel this way, if his kiss gave me more pleasure than any other intimate encounter, what would actually making love be like?

Click, click.

I inhale and pull back. Aiden's hand tightens on my jaw.

"Steady, Seraphina," he murmurs under his breath.

"Problem?"

I turn to Dylan and give her an apologetic smile. “Sorry. It’s just…taking some getting used to.”

She waves a hand. “We got the shot anyway. Let’s try one by the glass wall.”

I stand, avoiding Aiden’s gaze as we walk over to the incredible view of Central Park laid out below. Taxis look like bright yellow ants as they crawl along 59th Street.

“Okay, Seraphina, face the park. And then Aiden, right behind her and arms around her waist.”

I can’t help it; I tense this time as the full length of his body presses against my back, as his arms circle around my waist. Strong arms that pull me flush against him. I want to sink into him as much as I want to push him away. The day is clear enough I can see the George Washington Bridge. I focus on the bridge’s steel towers as I force myself to relax.

“Did I ever tell you about the time I picked my first pocket?”

Aiden’s voice whispers in my ear. A quake travels through me as he gently grabs one of my hands and guides it from the railing to settle over his.

“No.”

“I was so excited I held up the wallet for Dominic and Cassian to see. When I turned back around, the man was standing over me with his arms crossed and yanked it out of my hands.”

The image teases a smile to my lips. But it also stirs a sadness that he ever had to live his life that. Sadness and curiosity. I know next to nothing about Aiden’s life on the streets, or his life before.

Click.

"That must have been hard," I murmur as Liam moves next to us and gets a close-up.

"Less than ideal. But there were good moments." I want to ask more questions. But not in front of Dylan or Liam. I also don't know if I'll receive an answer if I do ask. Just like the kiss, I know he's only sharing to help me relax, so I can slip deeper into my role.

"Seraphina, lay your other hand on top of his. Good," Dylan praises as I follow her instructions. "Now both of you look out over the park."

The camera clicks as I stare out over the leafy green treetops, the skyscrapers circling the lake and trails. I breathe in, then out, slowly relaxing back into Aiden. His arms tighten around me. Even through the material of my dress, I can still feel the strength in his arms, the heat of his body.

It's not just that I've barely been touched by a man in the last four years, although that certainly plays a role. But the real reason is the man currently holding me in his arms. For years I've harbored my crush, indulged in the occasional daydream where he'd smile—really smile—at me before asking me out for a drink. That's as far as I'd allow my dreams to go. Anything more felt disrespectful and dangerous. Why concoct a fantasy that would never come true?

Liam speaks up. "Got it. Let's have you two head inside and face each other on the other side of the glass." He grins. "Lovey-dovey."

"Like you're whispering lovers' secrets," Dylan adds, her voice lingering on the last word in a way I can only describe as sinister.

The cool air of the penthouse sends a shiver through

me as I take up my spot on the other side of the glass and face Aiden.

"He's taking our photo," Aiden murmurs. "Not getting ready to bludgeon us with his camera."

I sigh. "I'm sorry. This is just so strange. You're my boss and I—"

He loops an arm around my waist, pulls me close once more except this time I'm facing him and I can see the tiny flecks of gold in his eyes, smell the spicy wood scent of his aftershave.

"We're playing a part, Seraphina. Remember that." He lowers his head, stopping just before his lips brush mine. I keep my feet planted on the ground even as my baser needs urge me to close the distance and kiss him again. "Remember all the people we're helping."

I gaze up at him, at this man who gave me an incredible opportunity when I needed a fresh start. A man I've worked side by side with for three years.

A man I barely know, but I'm expected to pretend I love.

"Why are we helping all those people? Why New Field?"

Aiden's brows draw together, but he quickly smooths out his expression, doesn't even bother to glance and see if Liam is still taking photos.

"Does it really matter?"

I start to answer, but then I shut my mouth and look out over the terrace. I've never told him about Brett, about why I volunteer at Grace's Refuge or what led me to fire dancing. I have no foundation to stand on.

"No."

I turn back to him and give him a slight smile. Then,

slowly, I raise my hand up and lay it on his cheek. His eyes widen a fraction. At least he's not wholly unaffected, even if I only surprised him.

"Seraphina—"

"All right!" Dylan steps in. "A few more poses, and then questions."

A few more poses turns into thirty minutes. Thirty minutes of me clinging to Aiden's arm, gazing lovingly up at his face, holding on to him and looking over his shoulder at the camera as we wind our way through the lower floor of the penthouse. Each pose is more intimate than the last, each one requiring us to touch, hold, embrace. Hands together, cheeks brushing, lips nearly coming together again and again. Inside I feel like I'm about to combust even as I fight the oddness of having someone photograph every move I make.

Aside from that moment when I touched his face, Aiden is composed. He slides into each pose with ease, doesn't seem to be affected at all. I can't help but despise him for his control.

Finally, Dylan has us walk back out onto the terrace.

"Last one," Dylan promises. "Face each other. Mr. Hawke, arms around her waist, hands at the small of her back. Miss Clark, arms loosely looped around his neck and angle your ring toward the camera."

A wicked thought infiltrates. I try to brush it away, but it's insistent. Pushy. Petty.

But as I look up into Aiden's calm, smooth face, I let the thought take over and subtly press my hips against his while I smile at him. His fingers dig into my back as his mask slips and fire lights in his eyes.

Success.

My triumph is short-lived as he grows hard against me. Even through all the layers of fabric I can feel him pressing against my core. I bite down on my lower lip to stop myself from moaning.

"And done." Dylan chuckles. "With the posed photos anyway. Liam is going to get a couple shots while we sit and chat."

I drop my arms and step away from Aiden. He's staring down at me, eyes hard and glittering. My heart is pounding in my throat as I wrench my gaze away. I started it, and dear God, I want to keep going.

For the first time that morning, I'm grateful Dylan and Liam are here to keep me from making a stupid mistake.

"Of course."

We follow her inside. She seats us in front of the fireplace but with the windows at our backs. Aiden reaches over and grabs my hand, his grip a little tighter this time.

"So." I can easily picture Dylan rubbing her hands together. "When did this incredible romance start?"

"The office New Year's Eve party." I lower my eyes, as if embarrassed, but I'm steadying myself, mentally reviewing the lies we concocted before I open my mouth. "We've always respected each other. But that was the night we both realized our feelings were more than professional."

Dylan tilts her head as her smile morphs from pleasant to slightly mocking. "So you're telling me you haven't dated at all in the two and a half years prior?"

"I am." I hold her gaze. "Aiden has the most integrity of any man I know. He never once crossed the line in the time I've worked for him."

Dylan finally inclines her head to me. "All right. Let's talk fire dancing then, shall we?"

The interview crawls and whips by in equal measure. Dylan peppers both of us with questions about everything from wedding plans and the Violet Masquerade to my fire dancing. I drop both Grace's Refuge and Cirque Obsidian's names several times.

Aiden doesn't let go of my hand the entire time. Every now and then his hand tenses in mine, or I squeeze his for reassurance. Once Dylan is gone, we can return to the status quo. But for now, I'm taking every ounce of support he's offering me.

"We're drawing to a close, but I think we have time for one last question."

The hungry light rekindles in her eyes. Unease makes the hairs on my arms stand on end.

"Brett Sinclair."

I freeze. His name repeats in my head, beats against my skull as I stare at Dylan. I'm looking at her, I know I am, but all I can see is Brett's face, the manic anger that last night when he trashed the kitchen because I had gone with another secretary for a drink and didn't tell him. Feel the pain explode as he hits me. See the reflection glint on the butcher knife he pulled out of the drawer before I ran out the door.

"Seraphina!"

I blink, snap back to the present. Aiden's kneeling before me, my hands in his.

"Are you all right?"

Slowly, I nod. "Yes."

Aiden watches me for a moment, as if to reassure himself I really am okay. Then he surges to his feet and turns with slow, lethal precision.

"Get out."

Dylan's smile dims. "We're almost done, Mr. Hawke."

"No, you were done the minute you decided to use my fiancée's pain to boost your ratings." He walks past her to the elevator and presses a button. The door slides open. "You can leave with the photos you came for and any information shared before that last question. If you publish one thing about that man in that article or any other exposés you write, I will buy *Gilded* just to have the pleasure of firing you and ensuring you never work in New York again."

The color disappears from Dylan's face as she stands. "The public has a right—"

"To know Seraphina's and my story when and if we choose to share it." Aiden points to the elevator. "You have ten seconds."

Dylan and Liam scramble for the elevator. It would be comical if there wasn't a buzzing in my ears accompanied by the awful sensation of being trapped. Trapped by my own choices, by the realization that my past will come out eventually.

Aiden walks back to me, his steps slow and measured. He sits in the chair next to me but doesn't touch me again.

"Do you know about Brett?" I finally ask. My throat is so dry it feels like it's been days since I've had water.

"No."

There's no relief to be found. He knows a name. He knows enough from my reaction to surmise what happened. And eventually someone will dig up the sordid details.

"I'd like a little time before I talk about it."

"Of course."

I raise my head. His eyes are on me, anger still simmering. It's odd to see, to know the anger is on my behalf. Aiden rarely displays emotion of any kind.

I clear my throat. "We didn't have anything planned tonight, did we?"

"Dinner at Le Bernardin. I'll cancel."

I start to tell him no, that I can suck it up. But instead, I nod. The thought of going out, of having photographers crowding around, is too much.

"Did you have any plans for the next few days?"

"Work. Practice at Obsidian. Nothing else."

"You're off for the rest of the week."

I nod again. I need quiet. Peace. I wish I was somewhere I could walk outside without paparazzi lurking, but maybe I'll just spend the week in the penthouse.

"How about a few days in France?"

I glance at Aiden. "Did you say France?"

"Yes. I have a villa outside Cassis near Calanques National Park. It's on its own peninsula with a private beach. No tourists, no prying eyes. Then we'll continue on to Venice."

I barely hold back the hysterical laugh bubbling in my throat. In the span of two days, I've entered into a fake engagement with my boss who once told me the idea of marriage was "unpalatable," moved into his ultra-luxury penthouse, and just had my photo taken by *Gilded* for a magazine spread. Now Aiden is suggesting we jet off for Europe.

It's insane.

Aiden pulls out his phone, taps the screen and hands it to me. The villa is stunning. Two stories of ivory white with massive swaths of glass and stone columns holding up the walk-around balcony that surrounds the entire second floor of the house. The picture was taken at dusk, the rooms inside glowing gold and giving me a glimpse of the living room with its soft gray couches and the kitchen with its dark wood accents. A pool runs the far length of the yard with what looks like an infinity edge.

"You can see the bay from the pool."

I stare at it. It looks like heaven. But am I just running away?

"I know the last two days have been a lot. It's a good idea to go somewhere we can have privacy and get to know each other outside the office. Give ourselves a chance to breathe and come to terms with what's happened and what we're facing over the next few months."

He makes it sound perfect. But what will it be like, I wonder, to be secluded with Aiden Hawke? I'm in shock right now. Exhausted. But I still remember the chemistry between us during the photo shoot, the heat burning through me when he pressed himself against me. Will we both give in? And if we do, will I be able to pick up the pieces after?

Oh, dear God, stop! That's not what I need to focus on right now. Aiden has always held to his personal rules and guidelines. Yes, he's attracted to me. But that doesn't mean he's going to act on it, and I sure as hell am not instigating anything.

"That sounds nice."

Aiden stands. "I'll make the arrangements."

"Thank you," I murmur, but he's already left the room.

I turn and stare out over the city. I overcame the odds before. I'll do it again. And this time, I vow, I will leave with my heart and dignity intact.

CHAPTER EIGHT

Aiden

THE WATER OF the Mediterranean is so blue that it almost hurts to look at it. I come to the villa so rarely that the sight of the waves meeting the paler sky never fails to impress me.

This morning, however, I only give the water a passing glance. No, my attention is fixed on the woman lying on a chaise longue on the balcony. She's dressed in one of her new outfits: navy shorts with gold buttons and a loose white shirt tucked into the waist. One long leg is crossed over the other, sunglasses shielding her face.

We touched down at the Marseille Provence Airport five hours ago. The flight was quiet. Seraphina gave the hand-stitched Italian leather seats and polished ebony wood accents a quick look before settling down on one of the couches and falling asleep, waking an hour before we landed. I had my stewardesses prepare her a light but nourishing breakfast—herbal tea, white peach slices and soft-boiled quail eggs. Seraphina had forced a smile and thanked them, even made light conversation.

She never ceases to impress me with her ability to

engage with anyone, to make them feel heard. It's one of the qualities I've always valued in her as a secretary, especially because I don't always exhibit traits like patience. But as I watched her, I realized I've come to appreciate those aspects of her myself. When I ask her to be my sounding board, she listens. Gives me feedback, even when it isn't what I've always wanted to hear. Perhaps that's why I've been tempted to confide in her these last few days. That, and the weight of everything pressing on my shoulders.

I shake my head. Yes, there's a lot riding on this. But right now, that's not my focus. My focus is making sure Seraphina is okay and that yesterday's debacle won't have a lasting effect.

When we landed, the limo ride was less than an hour to the villa. I didn't bother with a tour—we could take care of that later. I pointed out the kitchen since she'd only picked at the food on the plane, then took her straight up to her suite.

It's been five hours. Between the travel and the engagement and Dylan's nasty questions, it's understandable that she would be sleeping. But I need to see her, need to lay eyes on her and make sure she's all right.

"I'm awake."

Her voice is soft, a touch more life to it.

"I knocked a couple of times. I wanted to check on you."

"Thank you." She turns her head and gazes out over the water. "It's beautiful here." Her breath comes out in a long, slow exhale. "Thank you for letting me just be for a bit."

"You're welcome."

She looks back at me, her sunglasses throwing back my reflection. "You look concerned."

"I am."

"You looked up Brett."

I nod. I can only imagine what life with him was like in the four years leading up to when he was charged with domestic violence. His trying to attack her with a knife had obviously been the catalyst for her to file a restraining order.

I believe in justice. And paying debts owed. But abuse is one I can't justify or excuse. Brett's lucky he got such a long sentence. When he does get released, I'll be keeping tabs on him, monitoring. If he violates the restraining order by so much as an inch, I'll take personal pleasure in beating the hell out of him before turning him back over to the police.

"Would you be up for an outing?"

She tilts her head to one side. "An outing?"

"A little excursion. Introduce you to France, take your mind off things for a bit."

I can practically hear the gears turning in her head as she contemplates my offer.

"Okay. Do I need anything?"

"A swimsuit. Meet me downstairs in the grand hall."

Fifteen minutes later, we're walking out of the back entrance onto a terrace that overlooks the small cove down below. A catamaran bobs on the small waves.

"A boat?" Excitement in her voice eases a huge weight off my shoulders. She glances up at me. "You know how to sail?"

"No, but I know how to turn the key and make it go."

Her husky chuckle elicits a surge of protectiveness. On

the flight over, I felt…helpless. Utterly helpless for the first time in nearly two decades. Every time I glanced at her, I cursed myself for following her that night, for dragging her into this. If taking her out on a boat makes her happy, then we'll go out every day.

We start down the dock, the warm Mediterranean sun beating down on our backs. She accepts the hand I offer as we board the boat. My jaw tightens at what's becoming the familiar sensation of her palm rubbing against mine. That skin-on-skin contact—thinking back to the photo shoot, how good it felt to hold her. The weight of her breasts on my arm as I'd wrapped my hands around her waist and stared out over the park. The way her eyes had dropped to my lips just before we moved closer on the chaise longue.

I let go of her hand as soon as she's on board. I can't think about the kiss. Cannot relive the moment when she came to life in my arms with such fire I wanted to tell the *Gilded* team to come back another time while I carried her upstairs and finally made my dreams a reality.

The aftermath of Dylan Greene's despicable behavior cooled my desire. Cooled, but didn't snuff it out. Not by a long shot.

I head to the bridge. I turn just in time to see Seraphina easing herself onto the mesh net between the two hulls. She lies down, stretches out, a slight smile on her face. The most relaxed I've seen her since Saturday night.

I steer the boat away from the dock. The Mediterranean stretches out to our right, pale blue turning to navy where it meets the sky. To our left, limestone cliffs plunge down into the sea, shades of turquoise broken up here and there by the occasional boulder. Pine trees dot the cliffs.

The wind is starting to pick up, creating small, white-capped waves as we sail east.

After twenty minutes, I spy an inlet. I turn the boat and guide it inside the long, narrow passage. The hills slope down to the water, covered in pines and scrub. At the far end is a crescent-shaped beach with golden sand.

Seraphina sits up as I cut the engine and toss the anchor overboard.

"Hungry?" I call down.

When she nods, I head down to the galley. I open the fridge and note the covered plates I requested be brought on board while Seraphina was getting ready. I pull out a plate and a bottle of Dom Pérignon. As I turn around, I nearly run into her. Her sunglasses are off, her eyes soft and her body relaxed as she brushes a strand of golden hair out of her face.

Stunning. And too close in tight quarters.

"Do you need any help?"

"No." Hearing my curt tone, I add, "Thank you. Relax."

I nod toward the terrace on the stern. She heads out and I join a moment later. It takes a couple trips, but at last the food is laid out and the rosé champagne is chilling in an ice bucket.

"We have Brillat-Savarin, a soft cheese infused with truffles. Beluga caviar and oysters." I pull the bottle out of the ice and make quick work of popping the cork. "Duck prosciutto, sliced baguette and fig jam. Wagyu roast beef sliders with arugula and truffle aioli. There's mini lemon tarts and macarons for dessert."

Seraphina's eyes are wide as she looks around. "And this is just for us?"

I smile slightly as I pour her a glass of champagne.

"You've dined with clients before," I point out as I hand her a flute and pour a glass for myself. "Dinner at Rao's, brunch at Gabriel Kreuther's."

"Yes, but those were all for work."

She picks up a wedge of the truffle-infused cheese and takes a bite. Her moan of pleasure has me gritting my teeth as I stare out over the sea.

"This is really good. Thank you." She picks up an oyster from the bowl of ice in the middle of the table. "You don't have to walk on eggshells around me, Aiden."

The sound of my name on her lips ripples through me. I wait for it to pass, evaluate just how much I want the answer to the question that's been haunting me ever since Dylan Greene stated that man's name out loud and I saw the stricken look on Seraphina's face.

"You flinched the first few times I touched you."

She nods as she scoops the oyster out with a tiny fork and dips it into a small dish of mignonette sauce. "It's a little strange having my boss hold my hand."

"Does it have anything to do with how *he* treated you?"

Her brows draw together for a moment, and then her expression clears. "No." She shakes her head fervently. "No. Nothing to do with him. I promise."

I ease back into my chair. "Okay. I'm glad."

A few minutes pass. I'm surprised to find myself relaxed. I can't remember the last time I left my laptop behind and put my cell phone on silent. There's the gentle roar of the sea behind us and the high-pitched twittering of a bird overhead. The cover over the terrace captures most of the sun's rays, leaving the terrace shady and cool as fans spin overhead.

I also can't remember the last time I enjoyed sitting

with a woman in silence. There's no need to fill the gap, no awkwardness, just contentment.

Seraphina sits back in her chair, a half-empty glass of champagne in her hand and a look of satisfaction on her face.

"That was wonderful. I'm impressed your team put it together so quickly."

I shrug. "I told them they had ten minutes and they made it happen."

She shakes her head again. "I've seen the wealth you and your crowd deal in. It's just a completely different world to be living in it for a little bit."

Her last words slash through my contented state. A reminder that what Seraphina and I have in this moment is only temporary.

"It's the least I can do."

She takes a sip of champagne. "Because you feel guilty?"

I can't help the half laugh that escapes. "I always appreciated that about you. Never afraid to ask the hard questions in the bluntest way possible while still sounding kind."

Her lips curve up into a slow, sweet smile. "I try. And?"

"Yes." I hold up the crystal flute. "I'm very good at throwing money at problems and watching them go away. But trying to fix what happened yesterday, make you feel better…" I shrug. "Emotional support is not my area of expertise."

"But you do give. Your foundation, the bonuses at work." She smiles slightly. "You're a much better man than you think you are."

I don't know what to say. She stands and moves to the

railing. Stares out over the water until I see her shoulders relax slightly, as though she's made a decision.

Seraphina

"I met Brett my junior year of college."

No going back now. The weight of what happened has been pressing on me, a weight on my chest so forceful it sometimes hurts to breathe. I hope that not only will sharing finally alleviate some of the pain, but that Aiden won't look at me differently once I confess.

"I danced in high school, which didn't leave much time for dating. College wasn't much better. A double major with a minor and the college dance team kept me busy. I had a casual boyfriend sophomore year, but we drifted apart. My schedule was so demanding we barely saw each other. I started to wonder if I was pushing myself too hard, if I was missing out." I glance over my shoulder and give Aiden a weak smile. "Ego is a terrible thing. When a football player asked me out after a game, I was so excited."

I turn back to the sea. I hear Aiden get up and move about the terrace. My heart's galloping. Will he leave? Does he even want to hear this?

I nearly jump when he appears next to me. He gently wraps his fingers around mine, holds the flute up and tops it off. I watch him, amazed by how relaxed he looks. Instead of a three-piece suit he's wearing a white linen shirt and khaki shorts. His hair is tousled, the lines that usually linger around his eyes smoothed out.

"Thanks." I watch the bubbles in the glass. "That first

year was good. Great, actually. Flowers almost every week, dates, movie nights. Looking back, there were signs. Exaggerating a play he made during a game. Getting this frustrated look on his face when someone contradicted him before he'd laugh it off. But I dismissed it because everything else was so good."

He stands there with me at the railing. Waiting, ready to listen.

"It started off small at first. Asking if I could change into a different dress because he couldn't bear the thought of anyone else looking at me the way he did. He phrased it just so that I felt selfish for wanting to wear something for me. If he went too far, he'd apologize and blame practice or his professors or his coursework. And then…"

My voice trails off. Aiden lands a hand on my shoulder. "You don't have to tell me."

"I know." Resolve hardens in my voice. "But I want to."

I want Aiden to hear the full story from me, not some newspaper or social media post. I want him to know my side, know why I made the decisions I did.

"A week before senior year started, he asked me to drop the dance team. We'd barely seen each other the last few weeks, and he said he was worried we would lose our momentum as a couple. That this was our chance to prove our commitment before graduation."

I can still picture him standing in our little studio apartment with puppy dog eyes as he romanticized cutting me off from one of my favorite things in life.

"I agreed. That's when my parents started to wonder if he was really the right guy for me." I take a sip of champagne, enjoying the fruity taste of bubbles on my tongue. Savor it for a moment before I delve into the worst years of my life. "But I wanted the dream. Marriage, kids. Those first few months had been good, so surely they were overreacting.

"It only escalated from there. We graduated and got a tiny apartment in Harlem. I got the job at the PR firm while he worked as an athletic trainer. He didn't like that I made more money than him. He'd yank my hand when he got upset or grab my arm, but would always apologize after."

Aiden's hand tightens on my shoulder. I lay my hand over his. Foolish, yes. But I need this moment of connection, need the calmness that comes from his touch.

"It was so gradual it took me a while to realize just how bad it had gotten. If I didn't text back quickly enough, he'd give me the cold shoulder for an entire day. He'd make remarks about friends of mine implying they weren't good enough for me or had it out for him. I was so anxious, so unsure, I thought I was going crazy."

My voice breaks on the last word.

"That's what abusers do," Aiden murmurs. "They're masters of manipulation."

Startled, I look up at him. "Did…do you…?"

"My father abused my mother. I remember a little."

His voice is devoid of any noticeable emotion. But I still note his quieter tone, the tight clipping of his words. Whatever happened in his childhood home is still very painful.

"I'm sorry."

"Me, too." He meets my gaze. "You got away."

I nod. "I did. The last six months were terrible. Thankfully we weren't intimate. It was as if once he knew he had control he lost interest. I didn't have any friends left and barely spoke to my parents. His verbal abuse escalated. He'd grab me harder, started leaving bruises. He'd apologize with flowers or gifts, tell me he loved me so much he just couldn't help it sometimes.

"I finally accepted I needed to leave. A secretary at my firm invited me out for a drink. I texted him that I would be home late. When I came in, he was…angry." That doesn't even begin to describe the sheer fury vibrating through him. "He hit me. Accused me of cheating. I finally broke, told him I was done." My voice dulls. "That's when he pulled out the knife."

Aiden turns me around, plucks the champagne glass from my hand and sets it down before pulling me into his arms. I don't hesitate to wrap my arms around his neck and hold on as emotions sweep through me. Fear, sadness, embarrassment, relief.

"You're safe."

I inhale the scent of him, smoky wood and spice and a soothing hint of sandalwood.

"I ran. I didn't stop running until I got to Grace's Refuge."

His arms tighten around me. "That's why you asked for the building."

I nod. "They gave me a place to stay. Helped me talk to the police and sat with me while I filed for a restraining order. One of their advocates helped me find my apartment, and another introduced me to Cirque Obsidian. Jessica had taught some classes at the shelter before, and when the advocate learned how much I used to dance, she encouraged me to take it up again."

"What about your parents? The police?"

I scrunch my eyes tight to prevent the tears from spilling out on his shirt. “I didn’t want to call my parents. I was so ashamed. Another woman at work suspected what was happening and had given me the card for the shelter. It might sound stupid, but when I ran out of the apartment, all I could think about was getting there.”

He cradles the back of my head in one hand and presses me closer. “It doesn’t sound stupid. Fear makes us do odd things.”

“The shelter encouraged me to contact my parents. When I did, they came straight down.” My voice grows thick. “They never once judged me. They didn’t rub it in my face. They just…loved me. I got the restraining order, signed the lease on my new apartment, and then my parents took me to Maine for a week.”

Another shudder creeps down my spine, stronger than the last.

“We got a call on the third day that a neighbor had reported a man lurking about. Brett made parole and followed us to Maine. When the police picked him up, they found a gun in his car, along with duct tape and rope.”

Aiden leans back, holding me by my shoulders. His earthy eyes are burning with anger.

“If he ever gets out, I will make sure he never touches a single hair on your head or harms anyone you love.”

I believe him. What a wonderful thing to be able to do, I think with a small smile.

“Thank you. He still has years before he’s up for parole.”

“I don’t care.” He cups my face in his hands. “I will not let him hurt you.”

I stare up at him, at this man I used to think had no heart. But here he is, swearing a lifetime of protection for me, his secretary. He listened to my entire story and is still standing in front of me. No disgust, no turning away.

"After all that," he murmurs, "do you still want marriage? Kids?"

I nod. "I do. I've wanted it for a long time. I'm nervous about dating, whether my past will be a sore point. But I'm not going to let him ruin that for me."

Although sharing what happened, receiving this kind of support, has left me feeling lighter than I have in years. I've talked things through with my counselor several times. My parents, too, although I glossed over some of the details to spare them any further pain. Jessica knows some of what happened, but Aiden is the first person I've shared everything with.

"Any man who doesn't want to date you because of what happened is an idiot." Aiden's voice whips out, harsh and guttural. "They wouldn't deserve you."

My eyes drop down to his mouth. With the tension gone, my desire is returning tenfold. Suddenly all I can think about is the way his arms wrapped about my waist, how he kissed me, how he responded to my teasing and showed me just how much he wanted me.

"Aiden."

His eyes darken as his nostrils flare. He leans down. Anticipation builds as my body hums to life, ready to be kissed again the way he kissed me back in New York.

And then he stops. I can see the indecision on his face, the struggle.

Guilt floods me. What am I doing? Tempting my boss when he made it clear he wanted to keep our arrangement in name only? That crossing that boundary would violate his own ethics?

"I'm sorry." I step out of his arms. "I…sorry. Just a lot of emotions and I—"

"You don't need to apologize."

"Yes, I do." I rub a hand over my face. "Let's forget about it, okay? I'll grab dessert—"

I'm suddenly spun around and tugged against Aiden's muscular chest.

"Do you really think I can forget the way you tasted? The way you felt in my arms?" He pulls me against him and I gasp as I feel him again, hard and pressing against me. "And then you look at me like that after sharing…" He shakes his head. "How can I possibly take what you're offering after that?" Hurt, I try to pull back, but he keeps me in his grip. "I don't want the first time I take you to be for any reason except that you want me."

Before I can answer that, he kisses me. Gentle at first, his lips so light on mine. Then, gradually, he deepens it, one hand sliding around to the back of my neck as the other skims up my waist and gently strokes the side of my breast.

I moan. He opens his mouth and inhales my sounds, stokes the fire burning between us with every intimate stroke of his tongue against mine. He tugs my shirt out of my shorts. His fingers skim over my stomach, tug down one cup of the bikini I put on underneath my shirt. When his palm cups my bare breast, I cry out.

Aiden lifts his head. His breathing is ragged, his jaw tight as he stares down at me.

"Don't make the mistake of thinking I don't want you, Seraphina."

He pulls the bikini top back into place, pulls my shirt down. Then with one last sexy, angry look, he turns and heads for the bridge. A few moments later I hear the grinding of the anchor being pulled up, followed by the hum of the engine as it kicks on.

I grab my glass of champagne and walk around to the bow. The relief I felt in sharing my story with Aiden, followed by his kissing me like I was his last breath, unlocked something inside me. I didn't even realize how much guilt and humiliation I've continued to carry.

But now, with his reaction, the first traces of my fears are disappearing. Like his kiss unlocked something I've been holding on to for far too long.

As the boat clears the cliffs and turns right, I glance back at the bridge. Aiden is standing behind the wheel, sunglasses shielding his eyes. His head is turned, giving me a perfect view of his chiseled jaw, the straight blade of his nose. The wind ruffles his hair, tugs at his shirt.

He wants me. Aiden Hawke, a man I've admired and secretly desired for years, wants me. The knowledge is both terrifying and seductively thrilling.

I haven't been with a man since Brett. I've held myself back, partially out of guilt and partially out of fear that once a man learned the truth, he wouldn't want me anymore.

Aiden's kiss knocked that out of the water.

"Don't make the mistake of thinking I don't want you..."

I need time to think. But every touch, every heated glance, every searing kiss is making me consider that an affair with my boss and fake fiancé would be a very good idea.

CHAPTER NINE

Aiden

THE STRAINS OF music reach my ears. Drops of notes that remind me of rain splashing on the surface of a pond.

I glance to my left. Seraphina's balcony is just around the corner. But I can't see her.

I force myself to look back at my laptop. I stationed myself here as soon as we got back to the villa. I also made one phone call to the director of the Hawke Foundation and asked him to set up an endowment fund for Grace's Refuge. After learning firsthand everything they did for Seraphina, and everything they continue to do for people in need, I want them to never have to worry about money again.

I forced myself out of the room at six to meet her for dinner on the terrace. The sight of her sitting at the table in another of her new dresses, a long pale blue gown with a black ribbon tied at the waist, had me gritting my teeth all through dinner. She must have sensed my tension because she kept the conversation focused on business, asking questions about this account and that investment. By the time we were served dessert, I was almost relaxed.

But then she stood and walked to the edge of the terrace. There was no back to the dress, just ties that I could easily imagine undoing. I managed to wish her good-night and go back to my room. Pulled out my laptop again and started answering emails.

I had no intention of seeking her out again tonight. But as more instruments join in and the music swells, I can picture her dancing on that stage at the botanical gardens, the way her movements flowed like water.

I close my laptop. Stand. My pulse is accelerating, blood pounding through me as I walk out of my suite and down the hall to her door. It's partially open.

I pause at the threshold. I know what will happen once I cross it. When she looked at me on the boat, tilted her face up to mine, I nearly gave in. Nearly stripped her naked and laid her out on the cushions.

One corner of my mouth quirks up. I've been fighting this attraction for years. The last few days have been torture. But once she trusted me with her story, once she looked at me with the full strength of desire in her eyes, there was only one answer as to whether we would end up in bed.

But I meant what I said. I wasn't going to take her fresh off her confession. Not with her emotions running so high. When we come together, I don't want the past between us. Only the present.

I ease the door open and step inside. A palatial suite that mirrors mine, with a round bed on a marble dais and a gauzy canopy held up by slim Corinthian columns. Ivory furniture decorated with azure-colored throw pillows and silk blankets.

And a half-circle balcony that overlooks the ocean.

The lights on the railing cast a golden glow as Seraphina dances.

Her moves are light and graceful as she moves about the terrace. She changed into a loose, flowing dress. The pale purple reminds me of the lavender growing in the fields just beyond the villa as she dips, spins on the ground and then comes back up, pausing with one leg extended behind her. Her fire dancing was mesmerizing, but seeing the true extent of her dance training is captivating in its own way.

I want her. Need her. But I need to confirm she understands there is no future for us. Only these few months we have before we go back to the way we were before.

Warning whispers across the back of my neck. If we cross this line, can we go back? Can I break my own rules, let down my boundaries just to have a brief affair with Seraphina?

Yes.

As the song draws to a close, Seraphina rises up on one foot and turns. Once, twice, three times, her other leg out in a perfect line. She stops suddenly, drops to the floor. Then, slowly, she raises her head and looks straight at me. Electricity crackles between us just like it did at the gala. Except now it doesn't just flare and disappear. Now it lingers, building until I can feel it snapping across my skin before it sinks into my veins and heats my blood.

How did I resist her all these years? How did I work alongside her without touching her? Seeing her?

The truth hits me like a punch. I didn't let myself see her because I knew it would be like this. Not just a casual fling but one that lingered. One that could hurt.

Seraphina stands, her breath coming in short pants.

"I heard the music."

She winces. "Sorry. I didn't think it was that loud."

"Don't apologize, unless I need to apologize for invading your space again."

She shakes her head, a small smile on her face as she crosses to one of the tables next to a chaise longue and grabs a bottle of water.

"No. I…" Her voice trails off. She raises the bottle and takes a long drink. "Before the gala, I hadn't danced for anyone for years except Jessica and a couple of the other people at Obsidian."

"So why choose a gala with hundreds of people?"

"I didn't. Jessica was supposed to perform that night, but her sister went into labor and she wanted to be there for her. The other fire dancers were at some event in the city." She shrugs. "So I said yes."

Loyalty is a trait I admire, perhaps more than any other, given what Dominic, Cassian and I went through together. I already admired Seraphina, respected her. But hearing that she gave her first performance in years to help out a friend, to see the evidence of how much she's overcome, makes me realize just how strong and resilient this woman really is.

"Do you dance?"

I arch a brow. "Do I look like I dance?"

"You must dance at least once at the masquerade." Her eyes widen as I shake my head. "Seriously?"

"Seriously." I tilt my head. "You could teach me."

Excitement sparks in her eyes, but disappears just as quickly.

"If it's too much—"

"No. It's just…" She glances down at the ground, then

looks back up at me. "I haven't taught in a long time. But talking to you on the boat..." Her lips curve up. "I didn't realize how much I'd been afraid to talk about what happened. It kept me from dating, kept me from fully embracing my dancing. But you accepting what happened helped. A lot. I feel lighter than I have in a long time." She smiles. "That's a long, complicated way of saying I'd like to teach you."

I'm glad I helped. I am. But I also don't know how to accept her gratitude, her continuing kindness and the trust she's placing in me. I was always impressed by Seraphina's professionalism and how she never once showed any interest in me romantically. I'm starting to wonder if that's because she's only recently started seeing me differently or if she was just adhering to the boundaries I set in place. If I've been missing out on this side of a woman who's invested so much of herself into my firm.

For the first time, my walls no longer feel secure. They feel like a prison.

Seraphina holds out her hand. "Ready?"

I hold up a finger and pull my phone out of my pocket.

"What are you doing?"

"Making a quick call." I dial. "Yes, Arthur? Can you bring up a bottle of Dom Pérignon to Miss Clark's suite, please? 1953 if we have it in stock. *Merci.*"

"1953?" Seraphina repeats as I hang up. "Like in..."

"Bond. James Bond."

She wrinkles her nose. "Is it still good after all this time?"

I can't help but grin. "We're about to find out. It only cost me two thousand pounds at an auction in London."

"Only two thousand," she repeats.

"It's a quality brand." I pause, then decide there's at least one thing I can share. A part of my past that won't let down my walls too much. "John introduced me to James Bond. When I was studying for the test I needed to take to get my diploma, I'd put on the older Bond movies. If John was in, he'd make popcorn and join me."

Interest sparks in Seraphina's eyes. "He sounded like such an incredible man. What was he like when you first met him?" Before I can respond, she quickly adds, "Sorry. I shouldn't have asked."

I frown. I don't like that that's her reaction every time she asks me something. I don't like to share, but I don't like seeing her withdraw so quickly.

A knock sounds at the door. I cross the terrace and Seraphina's room and open the door for Arthur, who's holding a tray containing the champagne and a couple of flutes.

"Bonsoir, monsieur. Votre champagne."

"*Merci*, Arthur."

I take the tray over to the table on the terrace before I pop the cork on the champagne and pour.

I hand her a flute. "If I'm going to have dance lessons, champagne sounds like a good idea. Ready?"

She eyes the golden amber liquid in her glass. "As ready as I'll ever be."

We both raise our glasses. The flavor washes over my tongue, layers of apricot and orange followed by tastes of hazelnut and caramel.

"Wow." Seraphina holds up her glass. "That's…wow."

"Agreed."

I hold up my glass. The lights on the railing make the champagne glow. Seraphina has done nothing but give since this arrangement started. All that I asked and more. I wasn't going to push her about Brett Sinclair. That she told me of her volition, that she trusted me so completely, means a great deal. It also leaves me feeling cold and petty, a petulant child who refuses to share.

Seraphina

"We met John when Cassian tried to pick his pocket."

I pause with my glass halfway to my lips. Aiden has always been private. I don't begrudge him that, and he certainly doesn't owe me anything just because I shared with him.

But the thought that he might be sharing with me because he wants to warms and scares me at the same time. Warmth that he would actually confide in me. Fear that if he lets me in, just a little, it'll make it that much harder to walk away when the time comes.

"Where were you?"

"Times Square. John whirled around and grabbed him by his collar. Cassian was only thirteen, so Dominic and I came running."

"Thirteen?" When he nods, I swallow hard. "Wow."

At thirteen I was riding bikes, taking dance lessons and going on summer road trips with my parents. I once thought Aiden's current lifestyle and mine were eons apart. But I realize now I had my own type of privilege, my own luxuries I took for granted.

"We came running up. Dominic was big even then. He got in front of John and tried to distract him while I pulled

Cassian away. But John wouldn't let go of Cassian. He told us we had a choice. Either come with him and get a hot meal, or he'd call the police. I didn't want to go, but it was January. Tourists were scarce, which meant wallets were, too. So we went."

"Where did he take you?"

"The Empire Steak House on 49th."

My jaw drops. "Isn't that the place with a gold-crusted steak?"

"It is, although I ordered a double rack of lamb, lobster bisque and baked clams." When I laugh, Aiden smiles slightly. "I ate every bite, but I was testing him. I didn't know if he was a creep or just someone trying to rack up his good deed for the day.

"We spent nearly three hours there that first time. Cassian did most of the talking. But John coaxed Dominic and me into talking, too. For nearly three months we met John for dinner. Every Tuesday night. He'd let us order whatever we wanted. But I still didn't trust him. Why would a man like him be interested in three screwed-up teenagers the world had forgotten?"

"So why did you?" I ask softly.

"Cassian trusted him. Dominic had even started to thaw. And the food was good. But around March, Cassian got sick. Really sick. Dominic and I scrounged up enough money for a taxi and managed to get the three of us to the address on the business card John had given us. A town house in the West Village. We stumbled out of the taxi and up the stairs with Cassian's arms draped over our shoulders. John answered the door himself and called an ambulance. Dominic and I protested, but John just said 'You three are moving in here. That's not negotiable.'"

It sounds like a kid's version of Cinderella. "Did you ever ask him why?"

Emotion flickers in his eyes, but it vanishes just as quickly before I can discern what it was.

"No. He told us that he'd been down on his luck in his youth and someone gave him a chance. He wanted to do the same."

"And then he adopted you. All three of you."

I've met Dominic and Cassian when they've dropped by the office, sometimes for business, sometimes to take Aiden out for dinner. Dominic is an icier version of Aiden while Cassian is pure charm. I can't help but smile at the thought of them running around a luxurious town house after surviving such a hard life on the streets.

"Yes, two years after we moved in. John paid for our college degrees. When we graduated, he gave us each a lease on an apartment for a year and one hundred thousand dollars and said the rest was up to us. We wouldn't get any more help from him." Pride fills his voice. "We made it. All three of us. Cassian runs his shipping company. Dominic heads up his own private security firm."

"And you have Hawke Financial."

"I do."

"Thank you, Aiden. For sharing."

A shutter drops over his face, as if he's just realized everything he's confided. I set down my glass and quickly move to my phone. I tap the screen and a delicate melody starts to play, followed soon after by a swell as more instruments join in. He needs a distraction.

"We'll start with the box step."

He sets down his champagne with a sigh and stands next to me. He watches my movements, mimics my footwork.

"Good. Now, time to add the partner."

I turn and step in front of him. He's still dressed in his white dress shirt and black suit pants, although he left the suit jacket behind. My gaze lingers on the base of his throat and the dark hair curling toward the top of his chest.

I look up. Aiden's watching me. One corner of his mouth is tilted up. He knows I was ogling him. But I suddenly don't know what to do. I want him. Not just as a fantasy but him. Not for forever, I quickly remind myself. Just for now.

But I'm scared. The weight has eased, but the fear still lingers.

"Tell me what to do, Seraphina."

My lips part as my gaze drifts down to his mouth. I love the way he says my name, the emphasis he puts on the last syllable. It makes my name sound magical, sensual.

"You put your right hand on my shoulder blade."

He reaches around and places his hand as instructed. My dress is held up by tiny straps and dips in the back, so his palm settles almost completely against my bare skin. I arch toward him, my breasts grazing his chest before I catch myself and pull back. I'm feeling just like I did during the photo shoot, this delicious pressure building inside me and I can't do anything to stop it. Each touch only makes me want him more.

And this time, there's no one else here. Just Aiden and me on the moonlit terrace of a Mediterranean villa.

"And the other hand?" he asks in a deep voice that ends on a faint rasp, as if he almost couldn't get the words out.

I hold out my arm. "We hold hands at shoulder level."

He takes hold of my left hand, his fingers wrapping

around mine in a tight grip that is nothing like what a proper waltz position should be and everything I want.

"Now we dance."

My words come out on a whisper, nearly drowned out by the music. We move slowly at first, then a little quicker in time to the music. All the while he keeps his gaze locked on me.

"Is that it?"

I can't help but grin. "We could add a turn."

He pulls me tight against his chest and executes a sudden spin. I cling to him, caught up in the whirlwind of the turn, the press of his hand against my back, his body against mine.

We stop. The music is still playing, but it sounds so far away, lost beneath the buzzing in my ears, the thudding of my heart, the shallowness of our breaths mingling.

He brings our joined hands up to his lips, brushes his mouth over my knuckles.

"I want you. And you want me."

"I do," I breathe.

He hesitates. "I can't offer more, Seraphina."

My desire dips. He's reaffirming our agreement. Once our engagement is over, we'll go back to the way things were.

Is that even possible?

I don't know if it is with everything that's already happened between us. Which means I should take everything that's being offered while I still can. Finally discover if my dreams match reality.

"Make love to me, Aiden."

CHAPTER TEN

Aiden

THREE YEARS' WORTH of pent-up lust and longing come flowing out as I scoop Seraphina into my arms and lay her out on the chaise longue. I cross to the wall and turn the terrace lights off. Security is tight, but I'm not risking someone lurking far off with a camera. Tonight is for Seraphina and me.

She watches me with wide eyes as I approach, her hair loose and flowing over her shoulders, her dress spread out around her like a flower in bloom. Even in the dim light I can see that same blush creep up over her breasts, her throat. I give in to the temptation and lower my head, lay my lips to the base of her throat.

"Aiden!"

The way she gasps my name is like music. I trail my mouth to her shoulder, gently graze my teeth over her skin before I move up to her jaw. I rub my lips over hers. She moves forward, tries to kiss me back. I pull back and smile slightly.

"Not yet, wildfire."

Her eyes flare. "I like it when you call me that."

"I liked it when you danced." I move to the other side of her face, kiss her cheek. "Actually, I fucking loved it."

She shudders, her body arching toward me.

"I was so nervous."

"I couldn't tell." I kiss her other shoulder. "I'd noticed you when you first walked down to the lake." I ease back, watch the moonlight dance across her face. "I wondered if it was you."

Her shy smile steals my breath. "You did not."

"Oh, but I did." I reach up, stroke my fingers through the golden strands of her hair. It brushes across my skin like silk. "Something in the way you moved. The tilt of your head." I fill my hand with her hair, pull her face toward mine. "I thought I was going insane."

I kiss her again. God, I can't get enough of her taste. Enough of the way she melts into me, kisses me back as if she wants me just as badly as I want her.

I reach down and grab the hem of her dress. I undress her slowly, savoring the process, delaying the reveal. When I finally pull the dress over her head, my breathing grows harsh as I gaze down at her rounded breasts, the slim curve of her waist. Moonlight paints her skin with a silvery glow as her nipples harden.

"Aiden?"

"Beautiful." I look up at her, let her see the truth in my eyes. "Absolutely beautiful."

I lean down and gently kiss the top of one breast. She gasps, then releases her breath in a shuddering rasp that shakes my control. I want to spread her thighs, slide off the tiny pair of black shorts molded to her hips, and bury myself inside her.

But I also want to go slow. From what she's intimated,

it's been years since she's taken a lover. A fact that makes the possessive streak I've developed grow even stronger.

I kiss the smooth skin just above her breasts. Force myself to stay on my knees as she whimpers my name. I've imagined her saying my name, just my name, for years. Now she's half-naked in my arms moaning it as I move my mouth down to her nipples. I capture one in my mouth, groan as she buries her fingers in my hair and pulls me closer. I finally release her only to trail my mouth across her skin and capture the other nipple. Light grazes of my teeth, gentle sucks, slashes of my tongue, she responds to all of it. Her hips are pressing against me, taunting me every time she presses against my cock.

I raise my head. "Do you know what I would have done to you if Dylan and Liam hadn't been in the penthouse?" I grab her hips and yank her forward, thoroughly enjoying the way her eyes glaze over as I push my cock against her. "When you teased me?"

"Tell me."

I slide one hand into her hair, curl one strand around my fingers. "Maybe I shouldn't tell you."

Seraphina, the woman I once thought of as mild-mannered, eases her hips back just enough to slide her hand between our bodies and lay her hand fully against my cock.

Oh, hell. Just the pressure of her hand on me has me feeling like I could come.

"I think you should."

"God, you're incredible."

I kiss her, take full advantage when she opens her lips and invites me in. I can taste the champagne, taste her, as she kisses me back. When she starts to tug at my belt, I pull back, cradle her head in one hand as I gaze down at her.

"I would have spun you around, had you plant your hands on the glass, and lifted up that skirt so I could finally taste you."

Her eyes darken. "I thought you didn't like the dress."

"I liked it."

Too much. When I turned around after hanging up on Cassian and saw her standing there looking elegant and beautiful and bridal, for a single moment I wanted it to be real. Wanted her to be mine. But Seraphina belonging to me would require exactly what I can't give: love, marriage, commitment.

So I'll give her what I can. Pleasure, luxury, the kind of attention she deserves. And after our ten months are up, I'll pull back, resume the relationship we had before. I don't know how the hell I'm going to do it, but I'll do anything to keep Seraphina at the firm.

Including letting her go so she can find the happiness she deserves.

That selfish streak rears its head and growls at the thought of another man holding her the way I am. Sliding his ring on her finger. I grab her left hand and bring it to my lips, greedy satisfaction curling through me as the emerald glints in the silver light. I move my grip to her wrist, guide her hand until her palm is facing me.

"The first time I held your hand outside the store, I didn't want to let go." I lay my lips against her palm, kiss the skin. "Every time we touched during that damn photo shoot, I wanted more."

"So did I."

I slip my fingers into the waistband of her shorts and

pull down. She arches up off the chaise so I can yank them off, leaving her clad in another scrap of lace. This one, however, is red. A vivid scarlet I can't tear my eyes from.

"That day in the dressing room," I say as I start to kiss my way down her stomach, "when the zipper was stuck and I saw the blue lace underneath, I wanted to watch the dress pool at your feet."

"I wanted you to strip me naked."

I look up, completely aroused and utterly enchanted by the now telltale blush creeping up her neck. I lay a finger at the top of her panties, run it over the lace.

"And then what?"

Her throat bobs as she swallows. "And then I wanted to undo each of the buttons on your shirt. Kiss your chest."

I slowly run my finger down, tracing the gentle swell of her skin, every muscle in my body tightening when I encounter her wetness seeping through the cloth.

"Tell me more."

I sound like an animal, raw and primal, as I stroke her. I drink in every whimper, every cry as I move up and down.

"I wanted to undo your belt. Slowly," she adds on a breathless whisper. "Then I wanted to touch you." She looks down, boldly meets my eyes. "I wanted to suck your cock."

The thought of her kneeling before me, one hand wrapped around me as she took me in her mouth, makes me swell. Her confession rips away the last traces of control.

"Later."

I grab her panties, yank them down and lower my head.

The word *slowly* pounds through my brain, but I don't listen. Can't when I can smell her, feel her heat.

As soon as I place my mouth on her, as soon as I start to kiss and lick every inch of her skin that I can, she arches back and cries out, her body shuddering as her hands grasp at my hair, my head, the chair. Every sound she makes spurs me on as I use tongue and teeth to bring her pleasure.

"Aiden!"

God, she's incredible. The way she lays herself bare to me, embraces the heat between us as she climbs higher, pressing her core against my mouth until she shatters again and collapses onto the chaise longue.

I stand, gazing down at her limp, nude body. I see now the subtle muscles in her arms from her dancing, appreciate the litheness of her limbs. She's not just incredibly beautiful but strong, powerful.

I slowly lean down and gather her into my arms. Not the kind of powerful I'm used to where I can wield money and influence. No, it's the kind of power that comes from overcoming the impossible and choosing to live again, of surviving the worst humans have to offer and still having a kind word for everyone she interacts with.

Tenderness sprouts, slipping its roots into my chest as I cradle her against me. She murmurs my name, her head resting against my chest. An unfamiliar feeling and one I've never felt for a lover before.

Ten months, I remind myself as I lay her out on her bed. I know Seraphina on a far deeper level than any of my past lovers. She's dedicated so much to the firm I created and is now giving up nearly a year of her life to help me. It's understandable that I'm feeling something more.

Seraphina turns and looks at me, her eyes limpid as a lazy, satisfied smile spreads across her face.

I will let her go. But for right now, she's mine.

Seraphina

Aiden stands at the foot of the bed, his eyes devouring every inch of my flushed skin. I'm still drifting down from my incredible high. I feel so wonderfully heavy as the last vestiges of my release twine through me.

But when Aiden starts to unbutton his shirt, I sit up.

"What are you doing?"

He arches a brow. "Making love to you."

My chest tightens. I almost wish he would say something coarser, less romantic. Small phrases like that make it far too easy to slip into the fantasy and forget that whatever is happening between us has a very firm expiration date.

I push the invasive thoughts away and rise up on my knees. Pure feminine pride surges inside me as his hands still on the buttons. He sweeps me with a gaze so heated I wonder if I'm going to burn up on the spot.

"I want to undo your shirt."

His entire body goes rigid, his eyes almost turning black. "Seraphina—"

"Let me." I move across the bed and reach up. "Please."

Slowly, his hands fall away. I undo his buttons one by one, note the pulse pounding at the base of his throat. I lean forward and brush my lips across it.

"You need to hurry."

Thrilled at the effect I'm having on a man who's usually so in control, I merely smile. His shirt parts, revealing a muscled chest and the dark curling hair I glimpsed earlier. I lay my hands on his skin, palms flat as I soak up his heat.

"You're at work all the time." I love the sensation of his hair scraping against my hands as I explore his body. "How do you have a body like this?"

"I swim," he grinds out. "Every day."

"I'm glad."

His chuckle vibrates beneath my palms. I rise up a little more and push the shirt off his shoulders. The move brings me to nearly eye-level. I stare at Aiden, the familiar brown eyes and thick brows, the strong nose and fierce jaw.

My heart thuds. I lean in and brush my lips over his. Faint like a butterfly's wings, a gentle caress that soothes some of the sensual tension crackling through me.

"Are you trying to kill me?"

"No." One more kiss because I don't think just one will ever be enough. "Just enjoying you."

He was already so tense I almost miss it, the way his body tightens at my words. I glance up at him, but there's nothing except need written across his face.

I reach down and undo his belt. My breath catches as I undo the button of his pants. He steps back, makes quick work of finishing undressing.

And then he stands before me, gloriously naked and wonderfully masculine. Broad shoulders, long, lean arms, a chiseled chest, and thick, strong legs. It's incredible to think I've worked alongside him for three years and never knew what an amazing body he'd been hiding under his suits.

My eyes drop down to his erection. I wrap my fingers around the hard, silken length, shuddering as his head drops back on a groan. I stroke him, slowly at first, savoring the feel of him in my hand. Then, as I quicken my pace, I lean down and draw him into my mouth.

"God, Seraphina."

I love the taste of him, how he swells in my mouth while I savor my effect on him as I give him pleasure. His hands slide into my hair, gently holding me as I move. I tease him, lightly grazing my teeth over the sensitive tip, long strokes of my tongue while I hold his gaze.

"Enough."

His hands grip my shoulders and pull me up. He slams his mouth on mine as his arms wrap around my waist and he yanks me against him. He swallows my cries as our naked bodies press together. My breasts press against his chest, his cock against my core, and the way he holds on to me as if he couldn't bear to let me go, send me into a frenzy.

"Now." I frame his face with my hands, my breath coming in short, frantic pants. "Now, Aiden, please."

He tumbles me back onto the bed, covering my body with his. My hands roam over his back, up his arms, around his neck. His shaft is resting against me and I lift my hips up, wanting him inside me, needing him to fill the ache throbbing between my thighs.

"Seraphina, wait."

Doubt floods in, takes control. Did I do something wrong? Has he changed his mind?

"Protection," he grates out.

I blink as my lips part. "Oh. I… I got caught up—"

"Are you on a pill?"

When I nod, he shifts. He presses against my entrance and I instinctively part my legs, arching my hips up to take him inside.

"I'm clean." His voice is like rough gravel. "I haven't been with anyone since last fall." He looks at me, the cords of his neck standing out as he fights for control. "Are you okay with this?"

My eyes burn. I reach up, one hand on his cheek, and kiss him as I lay one hand on his hip and pull him toward me. He groans against my lips as he sinks his full length inside me. My body clamps down on him as I cry out. I can feel everything, every stroke, every pulse of his heart against my chest as we move together. Pressure builds, deeper and more intense than before. I climb higher as our hands and mouths roam, touching, kissing.

I explode. My body shudders as pleasure spirals through me. I'm holding on to Aiden for dear life, my arms around his neck, my face pressed against his throat. A few moments later he groans out my name as he reaches his release.

Slowly, very slowly, I drift back down to earth. Aiden starts to move off me, but I wrap my arms around his shoulders.

"Just a moment longer," I murmur as my eyes drift shut.

"I'm squishing you." His voice is amused, warm.

"It's a good squish."

He chuckles and drops a kiss on my cheek. When he tenses, I open my eyes and look up at him. His brows are drawn together in a frown as he gazes down at me.

"Are you all right?"

I can see the shutter drop over his eyes, feel his walls come back up even as he gives me a small smile.

"Of course."

He brushes a kiss across my lips, but it's brief, cold. I lie there as he gets up and walks out onto the terrace, confident in his body. I ease myself up and pull one of the mussed sheets up over my breasts as he pours us each another glass of champagne.

He's distancing himself already. Even as he comes back into the room, I know the old Aiden is back. He hands me the champagne and I force myself to drink slow.

He told me. Warned me. The sex was incredible. So why am I feeling so low?

"Are you okay?"

He's watching me closely. If he catches even a glimpse of internal struggle, he'll cut off our affair before it even begins. While I'm fairly sure I'm not going to leave this arrangement with my heart completely intact, I don't want to give this up. I've never experienced this kind of pleasure or intimacy before. Even though I'm struggling right now, I also know this will help me. Help me accept I'm still desirable, still capable of experiencing pleasure. That I can have a real relationship.

"I am." I slip my own mask on, smoothing out my face as I give him a small smile. "A little worn out."

His eyes narrow slightly, but he doesn't push. He finishes his champagne before he pulls on his pants and shoves his arms into the sleeves of his shirt. I sit there, numbness creeping in as I keep my gaze focused on the sea.

He stops by my bedside, leans down and brushes his

lips across my forehead. Another quick gesture meant to pacify, not arouse.

“Good night, Seraphina.”

“Good night, Aiden.”

He hesitates, as if he wants to say something more. And then he walks out, closing the door with a quiet click behind him.

CHAPTER ELEVEN

Aiden

A SAILBOAT DRIFTS BY, its white sails puffing out as the sea breeze carries it down the coast. The sun is climbing overhead and turning the morning warm. But inside, I'm cold.

Walking away from Seraphina last night was one of the hardest things I've ever done. I wanted to stay, wanted to lie down next to her and pull her into my arms. I wanted to fall asleep with her, to wake up with her in my arms.

When she uttered those words, smiled at me with such easy affection even as we could barely keep our hands off each other, I slipped. Slid dangerously close to something I wouldn't be able to come back from.

I got caught up once more in our lovemaking. But after, when she made me laugh and I leaned down to kiss her cheek, I knew I was at the edge of that cliff. If I fall over that edge, I won't want to let Seraphina go. But it would also be one of the most selfish, cruel things I can do to her. I wouldn't want to share her, but I wouldn't be able to give her what she needs. What she deserves.

Which means I'd have to let her go while I pushed

through pain yet again. I don't want that for myself. And I will not put her in that position.

Movement in the yard catches my eye. My body tightens as I watch Seraphina walk down the path that leads to the villa's private beach. I should let her go. Should give ourselves at least the morning to be apart. But I can't. I need to check on her, need to make sure she's all right.

I saw the surprise in her eyes, the hurt before she slipped on that professional persona I'm starting to despise. I want the Seraphina who lounges on a catamaran and smiles out at the sea. I want the woman who so brazenly kept her gaze locked on mine as she took me into her mouth.

I stop at my doorway. What right do I have to see that side of her when I can't even share a part of myself? Yes, I confided in her. But just enough. I didn't tell her about covering Cassian with my own body, trying to warm him up as he shivered and thrashed under the stained blanket we'd found in a dumpster. Didn't tell her about the winter nights we huddled together in a dumpster wondering if we'd wake up the next morning. I picked the one chapter of my life story that has a happy ending. One that most people at least know bits and pieces of.

But there is something I can share with her. A story that might help her understand why things are the way they are. Why I can't give her any more than what I'm offering in this moment.

I walk down the garden path, past wild rosemary and slender pines stretching up toward the sky. Has it really only been five days since I followed Seraphina down a different path thousands of miles away? It feels like it's been this way for years, even as the moment I recognized her on stage feels like it happened just seconds ago.

I descend the staircase built into the hillside and walk out onto the golden sands of the beach. Seraphina is pulling a gauzy white dress over her head. My jaw tightens as I take in the backless red swimsuit.

"Good morning."

She whirls around, one hand flying to her chest.

"Aiden."

"I'm sorry I startled you."

"It's fine." She blinks, and then her expression is just as smooth and devoid of emotion as mine. "How are you?"

"Fine. You?"

"Fine."

We stare at each other as the sea rises and falls behind her.

"I wanted to tell you a story."

Her brows draw together. "A story," she repeats.

I take a step in her direction. "You were hurt by the way I left last night."

Her shoulders tense. "I was a little surprised, yes. But you made it perfectly clear—"

"No lies. Please," I add when her eyes narrow. "We shared a lot last night."

"We did," she replies carefully. "But I don't have any expectations, Aiden. I told you that. You've been nothing but up-front with me since the beginning, and I'm still hopeful that one day I'll meet the right man and get married and have a family of my own."

She's saying the same things I've repeated to myself over and over. Yet hearing it from her lips sends a jolt of unexpected pain through my chest. That and a desire to punch her faceless future husband square in the face.

"Still, you deserve an explanation."

Finally, she nods. "All right."

"Her name was Melanie."

Seraphina's eyes widen slightly, but she doesn't say anything.

"About three years after I ran away from my foster home, I met her in line at a soup kitchen. She was smart, tough and a year older than me."

I look away, gaze out toward the horizon.

"I fell for her. My hormones were raging. And she seemed to like me. I'd bonded by then with Dominic and Cassian, but what Melanie offered was something I hadn't even realized I'd been missing."

I don't say the word out loud, can't say it. Just thinking the word makes me feel weak. Stupid.

"She was my first. I mistook lust and infatuation for something more. Every time I gave her money, swiped food from a street vendor, I felt like I was taking care of her. Protecting her. Doing what I couldn't for my mom. There were signs there was someone else. Dominic told me she was cheating, but I wanted to believe he was just jealous. I started thinking if I could just save up enough, I could get us off the streets and we could have a life together."

So naive. So stupid. Even on the nights she stayed with me in my little tent at the end of the alley, a part of me knew she was using me. But I wanted so badly to have someone, to feel something other than the numbness I had sunk into to survive on the streets, that I clung to an impossible dream.

I shove my hands into my pockets and look at Seraphina. Grief and compassion are written across her face.

"Six months after I met her, we were hanging out under a bridge during a storm with a few other kids, including an older guy who kept looking at Melanie like he owned her."

I can still feel the ugly snap of jealousy in my chest as I watched him leer at her, saw the glances she cast him when she thought I wasn't looking.

"He started a fight with a younger kid. Said Henry had disrespected him. It turned into a brawl. A passerby called the cops and they hauled all of us in."

Twenty years. It's been twenty years since I sat on that plastic bench with the cold metal of the handcuffs biting into my wrists. As I listened to the police officer tell me that one of the other kids identified me as the instigator and that I could be charged as an adult because some of the other kids ended up in the hospital.

"Melanie told the police I started it. I didn't believe Dominic when he told me, but when she walked by me at the station and I asked her if it was true, she didn't even look at me. She lied to cover for the older guy, who was her boyfriend. I had just been a passing amusement, but when it came down to it, she didn't hesitate to throw me under the bus to save her boyfriend's skin. She came back two months later. The police had arrested her boyfriend and he got a lengthy prison sentence since he was an adult. She cried, said it was all a misunderstanding, that she loved me."

Anger flashes in Seraphina's eyes. Oddly enough it soothes me, knowing she's angry on my behalf.

"I told her that once she walked away, I would never

think of her again. When she realized I was done, she lashed out, told me how she only came around because I gave her money and was a decent screw when her boyfriend cheated on her. Said I'd amount to nothing."

She hadn't looked beautiful then. She'd looked possessed, eyes wild and red as she'd screeched at me. I'd simply stood there with Dominic and Cassian at my back and smiled as I'd told her to watch me.

I walk to Seraphina, but this time I stop with at least a foot between us.

"Whatever capacity I had to love that day died. My father abused me. My mother died. And the first and only girl I thought I loved betrayed me."

I reach up, the knot in my chest loosening when Seraphina doesn't pull back as I run my fingers through a strand of her hair. I understand now her fear of having a man turn away after hearing her past. I wasn't sure if she'd still accept my touch.

"I care about you, Seraphina. I know love and marriage work for some. But I don't do emotional commitments. Not anymore. I don't like to depend on others. I don't like to share how I'm feeling or what I'm thinking. I would make a horrible husband and an even worse father."

She reaches up and lays her hand over mine. "I understand, Aiden."

I lower my head, touch my forehead to hers. "I know neither of us was counting on aspects of this arrangement becoming real. I want to enjoy what we have while we can. But if you're no longer comfortable, I won't touch you anymore in private."

Even if the thought of it hollows out my chest and leaves a giant, gaping ache.

Seraphina lays her other hand on the side of my face. "I want this, too."

The words are barely out of her mouth before I kiss her. Tasting her has become an addiction, one I want to indulge in as much as possible. Relief pumps through me when she wraps her arms around my neck. Accepting me, my past, what I can and can't offer.

I raise my head. "I have a little more work to do. How about I meet you down here in an hour and we have a picnic on the beach?"

She smiles up at me. "I'd like that."

I kiss her one more time before heading back up to the villa. But as I near the top of the stairs, I glance back. Seraphina is standing at the water's edge, the wind pulling at her hair as she stares out over the sea.

I should be satisfied. But as I watch her slowly walk into the water, I can't ignore the whisper of doubt across the back of my neck that things are already different. A barrier between us that wasn't there last night when I took her to bed.

I turn my back on the beach and walk back to the villa, ignoring the dread nipping at my heels.

Seraphina

Venice

A gondola drifts by on the canal below. The oarsman, dressed in the traditional black-and-white striped shirt and straw hat with a red ribbon, navigates the boat as the couple in front of him gaze at each other. Just before they pass under a bridge, the man reaches into his pocket and pulls out a box. They disappear from view, but judging by the excited squeal, she's going to say yes.

I can't help but smile as I turn and gaze down the waterway. Stone buildings line either side of the channel, some in shades of ivory or earth tones, others done in bright yellows and salmon pinks. The rounded dome of the Basilica di Santa Maria della Salute stands above most of the rooftops. Gondolas, water-buses and sleek wooden boats maneuver through the greenish-blue waters.

It's been six days since the Hudson Springs gala. Four since the photo shoot and our sudden flight to France. And a day since Aiden came down to the beach and shared what had turned him into the man he is today.

I glance over my shoulder. We flew into Italy this morning and checked into the Aman Venice. Not into a room but an actual apartment on the fourth floor that includes a living room with a crystal chandelier and ceilings painted with works of art that look like they should belong in a museum, an in-room bar and access to the rooftop terrace.

Sadness flickers through me. There are also three bedrooms. My room is, once again, stunning, from the pale green walls and sprawling bed to the windows overlooking the canal framed by filmy white curtains. But the separate bedrooms are a reminder that no matter how much Aiden and I might enjoy each other's company, our affair is strictly physical.

My heart aches every time I remember his face as he told me about the girl from his past. Learning more about the trauma he experienced, the series of blows and heartbreaks, puts his wants into perspective. I understand why he doesn't want to fall in love, why he doesn't think he'd be a good father.

I understand it all. But that doesn't stop me from wishing things were different.

I sigh and lean back, closing the window with a quiet click. I don't wish Aiden was different. I respect him for who he is. I liked him before, and I like him even more now.

Especially after the jaw-dropping news I received this morning.

I pick up my phone off the bed and read Mona's text again for the fifth time. It's a long rambling message with numerous exclamation marks as she thanks me for the endowment fund Aiden set up. Fifty-five million dollars with a withdrawal rate that will give Grace's Refuge an operating budget of two million dollars every year.

He hasn't said a word. We've spent almost every moment together the last few days. We've been getting to really know each other. What movies we liked, books we read, places we've visited. Aiden's vacation destinations were much more glamorous than mine, but he liked hearing about my summer vacations with my parents, our trips to Maine.

We've also been thoroughly enjoying our newfound affair. Our picnic on the beach culminated in him carrying me up the stairs to his room and making love to me on his bed. After dinner he showed me to the library, where we ended up on the rug, completely naked as he cradled my hips in his hands and took me from behind.

But eventually he left. Just like he said he would.

I toss my phone onto my bed. I told myself I could do

this. Told Aiden I could remain detached. But the more time I spend with him, the more intimate glimpses I get to see of the man behind the suit, the more I'm coming to realize that my crush ran far deeper than I ever realized. Every minute I spend with Aiden is teasing those suppressed feelings to the surface.

The sound of a door opening and closing yanks me from my reverie.

"Seraphina?"

I suck in a breath, grab my phone and head out to the living room. Aiden is standing in the middle of the room, dressed in a charcoal gray suit with a black tie. He looks up and smiles when he sees me. My heart twists. He's been smiling more lately. He seems so much more relaxed, happy, even with the New Field deal still hanging in the balance.

"You look beautiful."

Another of my New York shopping spree dresses, a turquoise dress with a matching belt held together by a gold butterfly and trimmed with white lace at the sleeves and hem.

"Thank you." My breath rushes out. "Hopefully it impresses Mr. Randolph."

"You'll do great, as you always do." He holds out his arm. "We're meeting him in the hotel bar."

Five minutes later we're seated on a long white couch in front of a window overlooking the hotel garden. The walls are covered in red and gold silk, with intricate frescoes adorning the ceiling. A bartender in a black suit stands behind the bar, expertly mixing cocktails as he switches from Italian to English to French as he chats with guests. I'm sipping a French 75 and trying to keep my nerves under control as my gaze moves between the gold chandelier, the smartly dressed guests and the doorway.

Aiden is reclining on the sofa, a whiskey sour in one hand. To the average passerby, he looks relaxed. But there's a tightness in his posture, faint lines next to his mouth.

I lay my hand on his knee. "We'll make this work, Aiden."

His eyes flick to me. "I hope so."

I wish he'd confide in me. Tell me the real reason he's pursuing the takeover of New Field so aggressively. I have a feeling that whatever it is, it could also sway Randolph's opinion.

He sits up and leans forward, brushing his lips against my cheek. I stare at him as a silly smile crosses my face. It's the first time he's kissed me in public since our charade began.

"Thank you."

Someone clears their throat. Aiden and I both look up to see George Randolph standing next to our table. He looks faintly amused as he glances between the two of us.

"Good afternoon."

Aiden and I both stand and shake his hand. Randolph sits in the chair opposite our sofa.

"So. The two of you." He shakes his head. "Don't know how I missed it."

"I'm sorry." Aiden tenses slightly, but I plunge in. I know Randolph's dossier like the back of my hand, know what he and his campaign managers are focusing on. "Once we realized how we felt about each other, we wanted some time and privacy to learn more about each other." I glance at Aiden. "We didn't want to announce anything until we knew for sure where our relationship was headed."

"Judging by the size of that ring, I'd say Hawke knows exactly where he wants this relationship to go."

"It's beautiful, isn't it?" When I look at Aiden, I let all my growing feelings shine in my eyes. "He's very generous."

Aiden stares at me, his face tense, as if he can sense there's a hidden meaning to my words. I turn away and face Randolph.

"I know integrity is important to you, Mr. Randolph. It was never our intent to deceive."

The amusement disappears, replaced by the bullish look I'm more used to seeing in our client meetings. "You must understand how those photos looked. The impact it could have if someone chose to capitalize on them during my campaign."

"And now," I add with a sweet yet firm smile, "your name is linked to one of the most prestigious wealth management firms in the world. A firm that is known for its ties to the Hawke Foundation, which just recently purchased a brownstone on West 86th for a domestic violence shelter and set up an endowment fund to maintain operations indefinitely at Aiden's behest."

Randolph looks at Aiden with something approaching respect. "I didn't know."

"That's one of the things I love about Aiden. He doesn't feel the need to publicize every good deed. He does them because he believes it's the right thing to do."

Randolph stares at me for a long moment. Then, slowly, he turns to look at Aiden. "And what do you have to say, Hawke?"

Silence falls at our table. Then, finally, Aiden speaks. "I don't know what I'd do without her."

Stunned, I whip my head around. Aiden is gazing at me with such admiration it takes everything I have not to lean over and kiss him in front of everyone.

"I see." Randolph leans back in his chair. "Well, now that that's settled, I'd say a drink is in order." He motions to the bartender as Aiden and I glance at each other.

"Does that mean you'll stay with Hawke Financial?" Aiden asks.

"I was skeptical. Very skeptical. The *Gilded* interview went live on their website on Tuesday, and my team noticed a change in the dialogue surrounding your gala photos. I'll forewarn you, Miss Clark," he adds with a slight smile, "that my wife has requested you join us one day for brunch so she can ask you numerous questions about your fire dancing."

My smile is real. I've met his wife a few times at the office. She can talk a mile a minute, but she's also very kind.

"I would like that very much."

His face softens. "But seeing the two of you here… I will be staying with Hawke Financial." My relief is short-lived as Randolph holds up a hand. "I'm not ready to make a decision on New Field. It's a risky venture. I'm not saying I don't agree something needs to be done. But it's a massive undertaking. One," he adds with a slight raise of his brows, "I don't fully understand your motivations for."

Please say something, Aiden. Tell him whatever it is that's driving you.

"Someone confided in me, Randolph," Aiden says, his voice cool. "The abuse they suffered is the tip of the iceberg of what's going on behind those walls. It's not just a savvy political maneuver and financially beneficial to your portfolio, but it would save lives."

A strong speech. But I can see Randolph isn't swayed by it. Like me, he suspects there's something else going on, reasons that run far deeper. That Aiden isn't sharing puts us both on edge.

"I'll have an answer for you in forty-eight hours. Meanwhile," he says as the bartender walks up, "a bottle of champagne to celebrate the happy couple."

As Randolph asks Aiden a question about one of his recent investments, I lean back and sip my drink. We're halfway there. Randolph is staying with Hawke Financial. He's still considering New Field. The whirlwind of the last few days hasn't been for nothing.

But as I sit next to Aiden, as he lays his hand over mine while he sips on his drink, his words echo in my head.

"I don't know what I'd do without her."

When our fake engagement ends, I won't be able to stay. Can't continue to work alongside him knowing how his bare chest feels beneath my hands, the taste of his lips, the feel of him inside me. Won't be able to see him resume his dating life and watch him go out with a parade of women.

I look up as Aiden squeezes my hand, give him a bright smile when he shoots me a questioning glance. I'll deal with my emotions later. For now, I'll focus on playing the role and doing whatever I can to sell our ruse.

A ruse that, for me, is becoming all too real.

CHAPTER TWELVE

Aiden

Glass trumpet vases overflowing with white gardenias and violet roses line the stone staircase of the Palazzo Pisani Moretta. I greet guests as they step from their water taxis and gondolas into the hall.

After our meeting with Randolph, I left for the Palazzo Pisani Moretta for a final walkthrough. Seraphina opted to stay behind and relax on the hotel's rooftop terrace. The night apart bothered me more than it should have, but I needed to keep my focus on the gala. And it provided a perfect opportunity for me to have one last gift delivered.

A gift she's wearing now as she stands by my side. The black halter gown had been brought over, along with several other evening gowns that would have paired well with a mask for tonight's event. But when I saw this dress in a storefront just off St. Mark's Square yesterday, I knew I had to buy it for her.

I glance over at her. The dress is comprised of swaths of orange, yellow and white fabric that cling to her torso and cinch at the waist before falling into graceful folds in a sweeping skirt trimmed in red. Diaphanous sleeves give her a mystical flare, while the matching mask shimmers in the dim lighting.

She looks like a fire goddess come to life. Primal satisfaction curled through me when I walked into the hotel lobby and saw she had chosen to wear the dress. That and my ring on her finger mark her as mine to the dozens of tuxedoed men who are eyeing her with appreciation.

Except she's not yours. Not really, a voice whispers in my ear.

No, she's not. But in this moment, to the public, she's mine. Even if that perception may not extend to reality, I wanted to do this for her. I can't recall the last time I enjoyed buying gifts for someone, of discovering something that fits them just right rather than opting for the highest price tag.

And that was before she talked to Randolph. I hadn't planned on letting her take the lead. But as soon as she started talking, I knew it was the right thing to do. She knows my clients, knows what makes them tick. I watched the older man's face as she spoke, saw him soften as she spun a story of new lovers just wanting some time to themselves.

"Ready to go up?"

She looks up at me, her eyes bright green behind the fire hues of her mask.

"I am." Her grin is infectious. "I'm excited."

"I'm glad."

And I am. It's like seeing the masquerade through fresh eyes. As we ascend the stairs, I allow myself a small smile. My mother would have loved this. She'd always dreamed of visiting Venice, of buying a jeweled mask and attending a masquerade. The proceeds from tonight's benefit go toward a mentorship program for foster kids back in New York. I started it in memory of her, to honor her hard work even though she never got to see it pay off.

The Grand Hall's walls glow mauve from the lights placed along the baseboards. Waiters pass through the crowd with silver platters of champagne, grilled scallops with black truffle dust, zucchini flower tempura and beef carpaccio rosettes. Several buffet tables are arranged against the walls, including a raw bar with a tower of oysters and a caviar and champagne station. A trio of musicians stationed at the far end fill the room with classic Italian songs as couples walk by, dressed in custom costumes or evening wear by brands like Chanel and Gucci.

"This is incredible." Seraphina looks up at me with shining eyes. "You've done a wonderful job."

Before I can respond, a hand clamps down on my shoulder.

"There you are!"

Cassian moves in front of me and grins. He's dressed in black trousers and a black vest with a maroon-colored coat that falls almost to his knees. His black mask glitters in the dim light. Warmth flickers in my chest. It matters that he's here.

I grasp his hand. "Thanks for coming."

"I wouldn't miss it for the world." His gaze turns to Seraphina, his eyes widening appreciatively. I bite back a growl. Cassian may play the field just as much as I used to, but I trust him. He would never seduce a woman who's taken. But that doesn't mean he won't flirt. A thought I don't care for as he grabs Seraphina's hand and raises it to his lips.

"Good evening, sis."

A startled laugh escapes Seraphina's lips. "What?"

Cassian points to the emerald ring. "Your engagement."

"Oh." Her laugh is a little more strained this time. "Sorry."

"It's okay. Busy night."

But I can see he's digging. He doesn't believe we're engaged. Part of me wants to tell him. But the fewer people that know, the better.

He turns to Seraphina. "Would you like to dan—"

"Sorry, little brother." I clap him on the shoulder. "The first dance belongs to me."

"What was that about?" Seraphina asks as I lead her onto the floor.

"He's being a nosy little brother." I turn and capture one of her hands in mine, slide the other behind her back to her shoulder blade. "And an outrageous flirt."

Seraphina chuckles. "Yes, I noticed that about him."

I frown. "Oh?"

"When he'd come into the office, he was always very charming."

"I see."

"He never did anything inappropriate," she hastens to assure me.

I still don't like the thought of Cassian flirting with her, of looking at her the way I look at her.

I follow the steps she taught me on the terrace in Cassis. Just like that night, I sweep her into a spin, savor the sound of her laugh as we twirl.

"I love the way the skirt of this dress flares out," she

says as we resume our box step. "It looks like dancing fire."

"How did you get into fire dancing?"

She doesn't answer for so long I wonder if she heard me or if she's just not comfortable answering. But then, finally, she speaks.

"I started at Obsidian just to dance. After the trial, I struggled with my self-image. I'd see the fading bruises and hate my body, hate that I was so weak I saw myself as broken, undeserving."

My chest tightens. The fury I usually reserve for New Field and its owner rears up, sends a quick spurt of anger flowing through. But her words resonate through me, too. It's like hearing a playback of my own internal thoughts.

"Dancing started to help me feel more secure again. One day I saw another fire dancer. It was incredible the way she moved, the way she balanced art and fire." She smiles. "The first time I lit a staff, I felt…powerful. It was dangerous, but I could control it. Practice, commitment. I loved having that sense of control again, of knowing I could wield it as I combined it with dance. And," she adds with a mischievous smile, "it's fun. Maybe you can take a class with me when we get back to New York."

"I already took a dance lesson from you."

"Just once, and if you hate it, I won't ever bring it up again."

The music slows. We stop our box step and simply sway to the music. As I hold her close. I realize this is the most I've enjoyed any of the masquerades.

And ignore that vicious whisper that reminds me next year I'll be alone once more.

Seraphina

I pluck a flute of champagne off a passing tray and take a long drink. The palazzo is warm and my dress, despite the filmy material, is starting to stick to my back.

"Congratulations on your engagement."

I start and nearly drop my champagne. I whirl around, letting out a relieved sigh when I come face-to-face with Dominic.

"Good evening, Mr. Hawke."

"Just Dominic. After all, we're going to be family."

My smile freezes.

"Well, Dominic, are you enjoying the masquerade?"

He grimaces. "Not exactly my kind of event."

"But you show up for Aiden."

Interest flickers in his eyes. "I forgot how observant you were."

"Sorry. I shouldn't pry."

"No need to apologize. It's a good quality to have."

"I can see that, especially in your line of work."

Dominic starts to answer, but his phone buzzes. He pulls it out of his pocket and frowns at whatever is on the screen.

"Everything all right?"

"Yes." He taps out a quick reply, his frown deepening as the seconds tick by. Finally, he shoves his phone in his pocket and redirects his attention to me. "Sorry. Client."

"Important to keep the clients happy."

One side of his mouth quirks up, just like Aiden's does. "Something like that." He glances toward the crowded dance floor. "I noticed Aiden looks a lot happier these days."

"I'm glad."

My eyes roam over the crowd. I finally spot him talking to several people over by a huge gilded mirror. As if he can sense my gaze, he looks up and smiles. Even from across the room I feel a tug in my chest, a desire to go to him.

Dimly I realize Dominic is talking to me.

"I'm so sorry, what?"

"You really care about him."

I still. The words are an echo of what I said to Randolph yesterday.

"Of course I care," I manage to say. "I wouldn't have said yes if I didn't care for him."

"A word of advice, then." Dominic moves closer and lowers his voice. "He feels far more deeply than most realize. He just doesn't like to admit it."

I lean back, not sure what to make of this statement.

"He doesn't share much," Dominic adds quietly.

"No," I agree. "He doesn't."

"He likes to portray himself as this cold, ruthless ass."

I can't help but smile. "True."

"And he can be. But he's also one of the most loyal, hardworking men I know. Just remember that when he's driving you crazy."

Dominic's head suddenly whips around. His face tightens as his eyes narrow on the crowd.

"Excuse me, Seraphina."

Before I can say anything, he disappears into the crowd, leaving me alone with my glass of champagne and my own muddled thoughts. I don't know if Dominic suspects our engagement is a ruse, or if he was simply making conversation. But as I glance over at Aiden, I know Dominic was right about one thing. Aiden does not give himself enough credit, doesn't want to see himself as good.

I take a long drink of my champagne as I utter a prayer that maybe one day, even if it's long after I'm gone, Aiden can finally look in the mirror and see the man instead of the monster he thinks he is.

CHAPTER THIRTEEN

Aiden

THE GONDOLA GLIDES beneath a stone bridge. An Italian song is playing softly through the speakers lining the boat as the gondolier navigates the waterways of Venice.

It's after midnight. The masquerade will go on until two or three in the morning. But after hours spent among the crowds, I found myself craving the quietness of our hotel apartment.

Seraphina is seated next to me, her head on my shoulder, one arm looped through mine. She's been quiet since we left, contemplative. Every now and then she'll turn to look at a passing building, but she's otherwise muted.

"Everything all right?"

She nods. "Just a long day."

I turn my head and press a kiss to her forehead. Her body relaxes as she utters a soft sigh.

"Thank you," I murmur against her skin.

"For what?"

"For everything."

Randolph bought our ruse because of her. Seraphina knew exactly what to say, faced him head-on when men with numerous job titles and fat salaries have cowered before Randolph.

"You're welcome."

The first notes of the next song begin to play. Soft at first, with the gentle singing of a choir. I freeze as the familiar strains flow over me, catapulting me back to a cramped, moldy apartment and a scratchy record player on the floor.

I can see my mom so clearly, standing at the window and looking out across the trash-strewn courtyard of our apartment. Can see the dreamy look on her face as Luciano Pavarotti's voice swells to impossible heights. I remember how she reached down and scooped David into her arms and swung him about the apartment, his little giggles filling that wretched space with a moment of happiness.

"Aiden?"

Emotion chokes me. My arm tightens around Seraphina.

"This song."

She leans into me, wraps her arm around my waist and holds me. Doesn't push, doesn't ask questions. Just listens to the music as we drift down the canal.

Pavarotti's voice crescendos. Crests. I exhale sharply as the song ends.

"My mother's favorite song." I shut my eyes, struggle for composure. "She always wanted to come to Venice. Buy a mask and go to a masquerade."

A long moment passes, filled by the gentle lap of water against the hull, the next song starting to play.

"The masquerade is for your mother."

Of course Seraphina would make the connection. It matters that she does. I pull her tighter against me.

"Yes. She deserved a far better life than she got." I hesitate. The words rise up again, the need to tell her. "So did my brother. My biological brother. He's the reason I want to shut down New Field."

"I didn't know you had a brother."

"David." Even just saying his name out loud hurts. Waves of guilt crash over me. "When Mom died, we were put into separate foster homes. I promised him I'd find him, but by the time John adopted me and I had the money and resources to look, he'd run away just like I had. He popped up every now and then in the juvenile system for shoplifting or getting into a fight. But he was always gone before I could get to him.

"Two years after I graduated college, I found out he'd stolen a car. He crossed state lines and hit a semitruck, injuring the driver. The driver survived with a broken wrist and a concussion, but David's crime and his past juvenile record led to a federal sentence."

"New Field," Seraphina murmurs.

"Not at first. But after a few years the prison he was at went over capacity. David was one of the ones transferred." I swallow back the fury, focus on getting the words out. "I visited him at the first prison. He barely wanted to talk to me. But once he was sent to New Field, he vanished. My letters were returned, my calls went unanswered, and they wouldn't let me in to see him.

"Six months later, I got a call that David was at a hospital. When I walked in, I couldn't even tell it was him. He looked like a skeleton."

Seraphina tightens her grip on me, offers me a physical lifeline I grab on to with both hands as I relive one of the worst moments of my life.

“He’d been caught in a prison riot. Broke his leg and was thrown into solitary for standing up to one of the guards who was beating prisoners. They left him in there for three days without food or water. Didn’t even set his leg.”

“My God, Aiden.”

The horror in Seraphina’s voice matches mine when I saw the extent of my little brother’s injuries.

“He made a mistake. A horrible mistake, and one he had to pay for. But not like that.”

“No,” she echoes softly. “Not like that.”

“They released him on parole earlier. Tried to cover up their mistakes. I paid for his medical bills and physical therapy.” I scoff. “Throwing money at problems.”

“Stop.” Seraphina pulls back slightly. “Do you have any idea how many people wouldn’t have even done that? Where is David now?”

“South Carolina. He works at a horse farm.”

“And I bet you offered him a penthouse in New York.”

I did, but I’m not about to admit to it. “He wanted to start over. He wanted a quiet life away from the city. I did what I could to make it possible.”

“Do you still see him?”

“About once a month. We’re both reserved. I think it’s hard for us to see each other more than that and be reminded of our pasts.”

Not to mention the overwhelming guilt I feel whenever I hear his voice.

“What about New Field?”

“I filed complaints, spoke with lawmakers, offered

Hale triple what the prison cost. But the sadist likes what he does, and his ties are deep. He has friends in the highest levels of government. He threatened to feed David to the wolves if I went to the media, advertise his record so he'd never have a chance at a normal life while spinning it that I was trying to make money off a prison."

"That's why you went to Randolph," Seraphina says.

"Yes. Hale backed me into a corner." I look down at her, anger sharpening my voice. "But he's not going to win."

She meets my gaze, an answering anger in her green eyes. "No, he won't."

I stare down at her, at this woman who's now heard the worst of me. Who's still sitting next to me and looking at me like she trusts me. Like she believes in me.

And God, I want everything she's offering.

The gondola pulls into the dock outside the Aman Venice. I get out, then help Seraphina, picking up the voluminous folds of her gown so they don't dip into the canal. After tipping the gondolier and the concierge on the dock, I lean down and swoop Seraphina into my arms.

"Aiden!" She laughs as she loops her arms around my neck. "What are you doing?"

"Carrying you to our room."

I walk across the tiled entryway and up the stone stairs, passing underneath painted ceilings and grand chandeliers as I make my way to the elevator. Our ride up is thankfully uninterrupted. As soon as we get to our suite, I kick the door shut behind me, set her on her feet and press her against the door.

"You look incredible."

Her eyes soften just before I kiss her. I growl as she

kisses me back with a fervor I've never experienced before, her hands sliding into my hair.

I lift my head. "The dress."

She blinks. "What about it?"

"Off." I reach for the zipper. "It needs to come off now."

Urgent need churns through me as I unzip the dress, push it from her shoulders and watch it pool into a heap of red and yellow at her feet. She stands there in tiny black panties and nothing else. A phoenix rising from the flames and ashes. So strong. So beautiful. So giving.

You don't deserve her.

The thought whispers through me. But selfish bastard that I am, I ignore it.

"I need you." I grab her hips, yank her against me. "Now."

I slide my hands under her thighs, lift her up. She wraps her legs around my waist and her arms around my neck as I carry her from the living room to my room. I need her, need to feel her wet heat, need to claim her in my bed.

I lay her down gently before ripping off my own tuxedo. I climb onto the bed, trailing kisses from her ankle up her leg to her thigh, stopping to drop a soft kiss on her core before I continue upward. I kiss each of her breasts, and then I'm nestled between her thighs, her heat nearly burning my cock.

"Seraphina."

She reaches between us, wraps her fingers around me and guides me inside. I nearly come right then as her body tightens around me. She moves with me, matching me stroke for stroke as pleasure burns in her eyes. Her fingers roam up and down my back, leaving trails of fire burning across my skin.

Her breathing quickens. The thrust of her hips becomes more erratic as her fingernails dig into my shoulders.

"Yes." I lean down and kiss her. "Come for me, Seraphina," I murmur against her mouth. "Give me everything."

She comes apart in my arms. I drink in her cries, glorify in her body shuddering beneath mine. Pressure builds at the base of my spine as my own pleasure intensifies. I groan as I come, pouring myself into her. As I drift down from my climax, I ease myself onto the bed next to her.

I don't know how long we lay there, bodies slicked with sweat. I finally open my eyes. And stare. She's lying on her stomach, her eyes close and her hair a golden tumble around her face. She has a faint smile on her face, like she knows a happy secret she's not quite ready to share.

Slowly, she opens her eyes. Eyes I've met countless times over the last three years. Yet I feel like I've just started seeing her, truly seeing her, these last few days.

"I'm going to start a bath." I reach over and tuck a golden strand behind her ear. I can't get enough of touching her hair. "Would you like to join me?"

"Mm-hmm."

I smile and move into the bathroom. I start the water and add a rose-scented bubble mix before dimming the lights. When I go back into the bedroom, Seraphina is almost half-asleep. I gently lift her into my arms again. But this time it's tenderness that fills my chest as she curls into me and sighs happily.

I step into the tub, ease us both in. Once the water's

turned off we lie there, her body cushioned between my thighs, her back to my chest.

"This is nice," she murmurs.

It is. I'm flirting dangerously close to the edge of that cliff. But I can't seem to stay away.

We lounge in the tub for almost half an hour, dozing off and on until the water cools. I carry her back to my bed and lay her down. She wakes up enough to glance around and frown.

"This is your room."

I pull back the sheets on the other side and slide under the covers. "It is."

"But..." Her voice trails off. "You like to sleep alone."

"I do. But I'd like to sleep with you tonight if you're okay with it."

Her sleepy smile hits like a punch to the chest. "I'd like that very much."

I slide my arm around her waist and pull her close. Her naked body curves into mine, fitting as if she were meant to be there. As my eyes drift shut, I have the fleeting thought that I could get used to falling asleep to the sight of her face next to mine.

I wake to a stray sunbeam lighting up the room. Seraphina is still in my arms, her face peaceful. I watch her for a moment, smiling as she lets out a quiet snore.

I've never spent the night with a woman, never woken up next to her. I didn't want to invite too much intimacy.

But as I watch Seraphina, I'm glad I broke my rule for her. I'm not sure what to do about the emotions she's stirring to life. Something I'll have to sort through eventually. For now, though, I'm simply going to enjoy.

My phone rings. I throw back the covers and ease out of bed, grabbing my tuxedo pants off the floor and slipping into the living room so the ringing doesn't wake Seraphina. I manage to pull my phone out of my pocket, anticipation building when I see the name on the screen.

"Good morning, Randolph."

"Morning, Hawke. Did I wake you?"

I glance at my watch and grimace. Nearly eleven.

"I woke up a little bit ago."

"Hell of a party last night."

I smile. "I'm glad you enjoyed it."

The hesitation on the other end of the line is my first clue that something's wrong. My fingers tighten on the phone as cold slips into my chest.

"Everything all right?"

"Look, Hawke, I've been doing a lot of thinking. I can't move forward with New Field."

For a moment, there's nothing but the thud of my own heart against my ribs.

"I see."

"I want to keep my account with Hawke Financial. But that proposal isn't a good fit with the campaign coming up."

I start to argue, to reiterate all the reasons why now is the perfect time to move forward and capitalize on his stance on prison reform. But I can hear the conviction in his voice. He's already made up his mind.

Should I tell him about David? Explain why this is so important?

No. There are plenty of stories in the files Seraphina and I compiled. Plenty of reasons why that place needs to be shut down. One more story isn't going to change his mind. I'm not trotting out my brother's pain and my failings just so Randolph can turn me down yet again.

"Thank you for letting me know."

"You're welcome." He pauses. "I'm happy for you, Hawke. You and Seraphina."

"Thank you. I'll see you when we get back to New York."

I hang up. Resist the urge to cross the room, throw open a window and chuck the phone into the canal.

There are other people. Others I can talk to, work through to bring Victor Hale to his knees and either destroy or restructure New Field.

But that will take time. More time, more money, more risks on people who might do what Randolph just did and pull away at the last minute. The happiness I've found the last few days vanishes, replaced by a cold ache. It's an empty feeling but familiar. Empty is better than rage, than pain.

A soft creak sounds behind me. I turn to see Seraphina standing in the doorway, dressed in my tuxedo shirt.

"Aiden?"

"Randolph said no."

She starts toward me, then stops. I see the indecision, the concern. I want to reach out to her, to tell her its okay. But I can't. If I don't keep myself calm, in control, the anger will take over. So will the pain of knowing that, once again, I have failed my little brother, just like I did all those years ago.

"I'll contact my plane, notify them there's been a change of plans and we're leaving his afternoon." I walk around her and start toward the bedroom. "You're welcome to stay if you want, make use of the hotel."

"I'll come with you."

I hate that that makes me glad. That a part of me is already so attached to this woman that her presence on the plane makes a difference.

"Be ready by noon."

I'm shutting down. Pushing her away. But failure plays on a loop inside my head. It was only a matter of time before our little getaway ended and reality came calling.

I don't look at her as I walk into my bedroom and close the door behind me.

CHAPTER FOURTEEN

Seraphina

New York City

AIDEN'S BODY SLICES through the water, his movements smooth and relentless. I watch from the marble countertop of the kitchen island, a glass of wine clutched in one hand and a book in the other.

Neither can distract me from the fury rippling in every movement of Aiden's arms, every fierce stab of his body as he traverses the pool. Back and forth, back and forth. An endless battle to combat his anger and disappointment.

I take a deep sip of my wine. Rosé, some rare vintage Aiden kept for special occasions. I barely taste it as I watch him swim.

I look away from my fake fiancé and stare out over the city. We flew back sitting on opposite sides of the plane as we traversed the Atlantic. The distance made it easy to slip behind my old walls. To wrap apathy around me like armor. Except as the hours tick by, the armor feels so tight. It doesn't feel like protection anymore. It feels like a prison, one that keeps me safe but also keeps me from a man I care about.

The L-word hovers at the edge of my mind, but I'm not ready to fully embrace that yet. I can, however, admit that my feelings for Aiden have gone far beyond my safe crush and ventured into a territory I've never explored before. One that terrifies me.

But not quite as terrifying as not giving it a shot.

Aiden plants his hands on the edge of the pool and hauls himself out. Water runs in rivulets down his muscled back. He grabs a towel off one of the lounge chairs and wraps it around his lean hips. His head snaps up and we make eye contact. Hope surges.

Then evaporates as he looks away and stalks to the door, anger still vibrating off him. He tugs the sliding glass door open and steps inside. His hair's slicked back from his face, his mouth set in a thin line.

"You didn't have to stay up."

I steel myself against the coldness in his voice. I'm not letting him push me away this time.

"I wanted to."

He stalks to the liquor pantry and disappears inside, reappearing a moment later with a decanter halfway filled with what I'm guessing is brandy. The amber liquid sparkles as he pours a generous amount into a crystal glass. I wait until he's taken his first sip before I speak.

"There are other ways, Aiden." I clear my throat. "Have you thought about telling Randolph about David?"

He grabs the glass and stalks back over to the window. "We're not talking about this."

Hurt grabs me in a tight grip. But instead of disappearing up to my room, I set my glass and the book down and slide off the stepstool. Dominic's words echo through my mind as I approach him slowly, the way one might a wounded animal.

"He feels far more deeply than most realize. He just doesn't like to admit it."

I stop a couple feet behind him. His head is bowed, his face shrouded in shadow. One hand is braced on the window, the other wrapped around his glass. The muscles in his back are tense, each line so taut it looks like he could have been carved out of stone.

I curl my own hands into fists. He's made it clear he's not ready for physical comfort.

"Not talking about this now? Or ever?"

"Drop it, Seraphina."

Anger swells inside me. "If you need time, Aiden, fine. But I know how important this deal was to you. It was important to me, too."

He whips around, eyes sparkling with fury. "It's not just a business deal. It's so much more than that."

"I know!" I run a hand through my hair as I try to sort through my words, try to make sure I don't stick my foot in my mouth and push him even further away. "I'm not saying I can even begin to comprehend your disappointment and anger. I just wanted to say it was important to me, too, and if Randolph said no, then we just need to—"

"There is no 'we.'"

The world drops out from beneath my feet. I'm standing here, staring at Aiden, but it feels as if I'm falling through space.

"I see."

Everything I thought we had built in Europe—the camaraderie, the trust, the tentative friendship that bordered on something more—doesn't exist. Aiden is nothing like Brett. Which, I realize as I turn away and move toward the kitchen island to grab my phone, makes this whole situation worse. Ten times worse. When I ended things with Brett, the relief left me weak-kneed and feeling so light I half wondered if I'd float up to the ceiling.

Now the pain is immense. A stab that pierces skin and bone and cuts straight to my heart.

Because, I acknowledge, as my vision blurs, I am in love with Aiden. Perhaps my crush on him has always been more than the shallow fondness I told myself it was. Maybe it's the intimacy of making love with someone who pays attention to me, to my needs and wants and pleasure.

But it's so much more than that. Aiden is so much more than that. Learning about the man behind the facade, how he rose above impossible heartbreak and achieved success while still staying true to his roots, pulled me over the edge I've been standing on for far longer than I'm comfortable admitting.

I press my lips together. I will not cry in front of him. I will not let myself look like a fool.

"Seraphina."

The sound of my name, that guttural pain lurking in his voice, pulls at me. My traitorous heart leaps. For one moment, I wonder, *what if*?

Except that's what I did with Brett. For years. Aiden is nothing like Brett. Our relationship, false as it is, has everything I've dreamed about. Someone I can talk to, who listens to and respects me, someone who likes trying new things and cares about more than just their career or how good they look.

But the one thing still missing is the one thing I will

never compromise on again. I need more than just a friend and lover. I want, and deserve, a man who will love me just as much as I love him. I'm not settling for less, and I'm not pushing Aiden to give what he doesn't want to.

"I have to go."

"Go where?"

"Practice."

I pour the rest of the wine down the sink, rinse out the glass and pick up my book, avoiding looking at him. Tomorrow, I think. I'll break things off tomorrow or the day after. Give him a little time to process the blow from George Randolph.

"I'll stay at my place tonight. It's closer."

Aiden stares at me, eyes sharp and intense as he watches me. I resist the urge to squirm. I have nothing to feel guilty about. Nothing.

"How about I drive you and then bring you back here?"

"No." I clear my throat. "I'll just take a cab."

"I didn't…" His voice trails off and he looks away, his jaw so tight he could probably crunch rocks between his teeth. "I'm not asking you to leave, Seraphina."

"I know. I'm offering. Not just for you, although that's part of it." I take a risk and close the distance between us. "But for me, too. It's hard…" I hesitate. Try to find the balance of how much to share without making this all about me. "It's hard for me to be here when you're shutting me out."

He blinks. "It's not personal."

The knife stabs deeper, twists. I force myself to nod before I reach up and lay my hand on his cheek. The hint of stubble grazes my palm, sends a shudder through me. "It's okay, Aiden."

He blinks again as his brows draw together. Before he can say anything else, I lean up on my toes and kiss him. I only intended for it to be a quick graze of the lips. But it suddenly hits me that this is probably the last time I'll kiss him. The deal is lost. The media attention is dying down. There's no need for me to live here, to wear his ring on my finger.

When I walk out that door, we'll be over.

I move, sliding one hand around the back of his neck to pull him closer as my other hand slides up into his wet hair. I gasp his name, press my hips against him.

We detonate. His arms come around me and pin me to his hard, damp chest. He hardens against me as my thighs clench. His lips part. Our tongues meet, duel as I rip away the towel and he grabs the hem of my dress. We break apart for a half second for him to rip it over my head before we slam back into each other. Mouths, hands moving relentlessly, touching every inch we can as he walks me back.

Before I can catch my breath, his hands tighten on my waist and he lifts me up onto the counter, bringing me eye-level with him. For a moment I see something flare in the chestnut depths, something warm that makes my chest ache with longing.

And then it's gone, replaced by the one thing Aiden lets exist between us: desire.

So I take it. I take every tiny piece he offers and hold it close as he kisses me with such possessive confidence I can barely catch my breath. He swallows every moan as he unhooks my bra, trails his mouth down my neck as he palms my bare breasts, cradles them in his hands. He pulls me to the edge of the countertop, stepping between my thighs as he presses himself against my core. I can feel every inch of him through the thin layer of my underwear.

He hooks his fingers in the waistband and pulls down. I arch up off the counter, watch him as he slides the material down my legs, eyes never leaving mine. My body is burning, equal parts shyness and brazen need. I nearly close my legs, hide myself.

But I don't. I want him to see me, every inch of me. Need this last moment.

His arms come around. For a few blissful seconds, he holds me. Just holds me in the circle of his arms. I close my eyes and breathe in the scent of pool water clinging to his skin, the faint trace of cedar from his soap. Feel the beating of his heart against my chest.

I notice every detail. Memorize it.

Then Aiden grips my chin in his hand and tilts my face up to his. His lips slant over mine as he slides the tip of his cock up and down my slick skin. My mouth parts as he slides in. His groan vibrates against my mouth as my body tightens around him.

"God, Seraphina, you feel so good."

I wrap my arms around his neck, brazenly push my breasts against his chest as I wrap my legs around his waist and take him deeper. His eyes darken as his fingers tighten on my hips.

"If you keep doing that—"

"What?" I push against him, ridiculously satisfied when his lips part. "That?"

His hands slide under my rear and he lifts me off the counter. I laugh as he spins me around, then moan when he presses me against the wall and leans his forehead against mine. Our breaths mingle, harsh and heated, our bodies joined.

"Yes." His kiss is quick, deep. "That."

Every thrust carries me higher. I murmur his name, kiss his sweat-slicked skin, dig my nails into his back as I arch against him, wanting him deeper, wanting more, wanting this to never stop.

I can feel my release building. Delicious pressure gathering just above where our bodies are joined. I look up at him, cup his face.

"Aiden."

That one uttering of his name is filled with everything I feel for him. His eyes flicker, but before he can reply, I come apart in his arms. Sensation spirals through me, fire racing through my veins and over my skin as I cling to him, crying out his name over and over. He groans mine as he pins me against the wall and his heat fills me.

I don't know how long we stand there, Aiden holding me in the arms as his ragged breath falls on my shoulder. I gently stroke his hair, the back of his neck.

I wish we could stay like this.

I close my eyes. Savor the feel of him against me, inside me. Then, gently, I lift my head. Desire lingers in his eyes, sated pleasure relaxing his face for the first time since we left Venice.

But it's not enough. Desire and pleasure will never fill the holes reserved for love, a family. Aiden will never fully let me in. Our relationship will always be an imbalance, one where I will live in a state of wondering when he'll leave.

I choke back a sob. One day I'll look back on my time with Aiden and appreciate that loving him gave me the courage to move forward with my life, to stop punishing myself and start fully living again.

Now, however, it breaks my heart.

He lowers me to the floor and pulls away. I stand there against the wall, my heart beating a frantic rhythm against my chest, pleading with me to not do anything drastic.

But I already know this needs to end. Dragging it out another day or two won't make a difference. Slowly, I grab the ring. Aiden's eyes drop down, his body going rigid as he watches me pull it off my finger.

"There's no deal," I whisper. I swallow past the lump in my throat and grab his wrist. I place the ring in the middle of his palm. Already I feel naked without it. "So we don't need to continue this arrangement any longer."

His fingers close around it. Slowly, he raises his head. The tortured look in his eyes nearly undoes me.

"I don't want you to go."

It's like getting hit by lightning. Those six little words rip away my walls and leave my heart bare. I'm in love with Aiden Hawke. Probably have been for years. A love that has grown and deepened over the last week as I came to know him.

But for love to succeed, it must be returned. Aiden cares about me. But he doesn't love me.

A tear escapes, traces a hot trail down my cheek. "I don't want to go, either." I lay a hand against his cheek. "If I stay, we'll both end up hurt. Resentful, maybe even angry. What we had this past week will disappear." I give him a trembling smile. "And I want to hold on to that."

He doesn't say anything as I grab my purse and suitcase. I left all of my new dresses and accessories in the closet upstairs. I'll figure out a way to have them donated later. Right now, though, I just need to get out of here.

The elevator doors open. I step inside and turn to press the button for the lobby. Just as the doors close, Aiden looks up. Our eyes meet.

And then he's gone, leaving me with forty-one seconds to cry my heart out as the elevator carries me away from the man I love.

CHAPTER FIFTEEN

Seraphina

One day later

I TILT MY head back. Savor the warmth of the summer afternoon. Try not to think about my computer sitting on my parents' kitchen table and the email I sent ten minutes ago.

"Dear Mr. Hawke, I am tendering my resignation, effective immediately. I appreciate the opportunity..."

He won't reply. Which is for the best, I remind myself for the hundredth time. We're incompatible. The family issue is a no-brainer. I want children. Aiden doesn't. That he didn't want me to go matters. But if I'd stayed for any length of time, I would have placed myself back into a relationship with an unequal balance of power. One where I would be adapting myself and my needs to someone else's wants and comfort.

Walking away from Aiden was the right choice. Maybe, one day, the logic of my choice will make the heartache easier.

As soon as I walked into my apartment, I called my mom. I managed to choke out that Aiden and I had broken up. Three hours later we were driving out of New York City and up to their home on a quiet street in Millbrook. Mom didn't ask questions or pester. She simply drove with my favorite songs playing and one hand wrapped gently around mine. Dad was waiting when we got home. And they both did what they did before. Loved me. Supported me.

"Here we go."

I turn and look over my shoulder, smiling as my mother walks up to the picnic table with a glass in each hand.

"What's that?" I ask as I nod to the flutes.

"Your father brought back several bottes of gin from a distillery in Kansas City." Mom rolls her eyes as she sets the glasses down on the table. "Apparently his next career is going to be a bartender. We have here the French 75, a champagne cocktail with gin and lemon."

"I don't know what I'd do without her."

I swallow past the tightness in my throat as I slide off the swing and walk toward the table. "It's three o'clock in the afternoon."

"And you did something important." Mom hands me a glass and clinks hers against mine. "Something that warrants an early drink."

Heat pricks my eyes. "Thanks, Mom."

We sip our cocktails, the sweetness of champagne and tartness of lemon eliciting sighs of appreciation from both of us.

"Will Dad be back in time for the exhibition on Thursday?"

"He wouldn't miss it for the world." Mom smiles. "I'm so excited for you."

After I left Aiden's penthouse, I went straight to Obsidian. I danced for an hour, doing tricks with my staff, then my sword. I took it slow since it had been over a week, but I slipped back into it like I'd never left. Jessica stopped by to check on me. If she noticed my missing engagement ring, she didn't say anything. But she did surprise me with an invitation to dance at their exhibition on Thursday. Cirque Obsidian's first in-house event showcasing their students and instructors.

I almost said no out of habit. But when I thought about all the adventures I'd taken in the last week, from getting engaged to my boss to dancing at a Venetian masquerade, dancing in front of a couple hundred other students didn't seem so scary.

And it gave me an opportunity to correct a mistake. I invited my parents to attend.

"I…" I swallow hard. "I know I put you and Dad through hell—"

"Darling." Mom cuts me off, her voice firm and loving. "We loved you through all of it. Love isn't just about the good moments."

I think about Aiden, the pain in his eyes when I told him I couldn't be with him anymore. Grief chokes me. I know I made the right choice, but it only seems to make the pain worse.

"I…" I press my lips together, get myself back under control. "Aiden…"

"You love him," Mom says softly.

"I love him so much it hurts." My voice breaks on the last word. "It hurts so much, Mom. I had a crush on him for the longest time, but it was safe, you know? He was my boss, there was no risk, I could just admire his… well, his—"

"His great ass."

I laugh through my tears. "Mom!"

"What? I'm in my fifties, not dead." Her smile dims as she watches me. "You made the right choice."

"I did." I stare down at the lemon peel curled inside my glass. "His upbringing, Mom, was…it was awful." I want to tell her everything, but it's not my story to tell. "He's not like Brett. He respects me and he's so intelligent. I didn't realize how much he's tried to give back, how much he's supported his brother, and I… I…"

"And you love him," Mom repeats softly.

"I do," I choke out. "I do, but he doesn't love me back. He cares for me, and God, I want that to be enough."

"But the fact that it's not, Sera, shows how much you've grown. Matured."

I suck in a shuddering breath. "Does it? Or does it mean I'm not giving him the time and patience he needs to come around?"

"Unfortunately, that's only a question he can answer."

Slowly, I nod. "I'm afraid the answer is no."

"And it might be, darling." Mom stands, circles the table and sits next to me, wrapping her arms around me. "I hope for your sake, and his, he comes around. But whether he does or not, you stood up for yourself."

Tears pour down my cheeks. "What I felt for Brett those first few months we dated is nothing compared to what I feel for Aiden. It's not just lust or desire or some superficial emotion. Aiden supports me, makes me feel… seen. It terrified me at first, but the more time I spent with him, the more I…"

The tears finally overwhelm me. Claim what little control I managed to scrounge over the last few days.

"I love him, Mom." I suck in another shuddering

breath. “I love him so much. But he can’t let himself love me.”

“Then he’s an idiot.” Mom holds up a hand as I start to protest. “I respect him for being honest with you, Sera. He could have very easily lied, but he did the honorable thing. I call him an idiot because I suspect he cares far more than he’s willing to accept.”

I nod. “He told me he cares for me. And that’s one of the hardest parts. For him, that’s huge. Astronomical. But I want…”

“You want love.” Mom brushes a calming hand over my hair. “And you deserve it. You don’t have to accept what he offers just because it’s all he has to give.”

“I want children, Mom.” Her arms tense around me. “Even if I could give him time to figure out the emotional baggage he lugs around, he doesn’t want kids.” My voice breaks again. “I won’t sacrifice that.”

She kisses my forehead and hugs me tighter. “I’m proud of you.”

“Thanks.” I choke out a watery laugh. “Maybe one day I’ll be proud of me, too.”

Aiden

I stare at the email on my computer screen. The one that came this morning and tanked my already horrendous mood.

When I saw her email address, hope flared inside me. Hope that rapidly evaporated when I read the subject line: *Resignation Notice.*

I glance at the paper on my desk. A printed copy of the job write-up I had one of the other secretaries do this morning, one I could trust to be discreet. It should be posted now. My calendar is filled for the next four weeks solid. Without Seraphina here to oversee all the duties and tasks she took care of, I'm anticipating at least seventy hours this week to make sure everything gets completed.

Not that that's a bad thing. It's kept me focused on moving forward instead of dwelling on the look on Seraphina's face right after we made love that final time, the cold weight of her ring in my hand as she walked out the door.

I minimize her email and pull up another file. When I haven't been working, I've been swimming. Back and forth, back and forth, going straight for an ice-cold shower when I get out. If I stop to think for one second, I can see her as if she's there in front of me, those gorgeous lips parted on a moan as I knelt between her legs on the balcony and tasted her for the first time—

Damn.

I push away from my desk and start to pace. It hasn't even been two days. I just need time. It hurts now, sure. But it'll pass.

It has to.

Except as I stare out the wall of windows in my office, I know it won't fully pass. It will linger, flare at the worst possible moments, just like memories of Mom and David do.

Lights flicker across the city, turning skyscrapers and soaring buildings from simple structures of chrome and streel into glittering towers that stand out against the encroaching night. A sight that normally brings an immense sense of satisfaction, a visual reminder of how far I've come.

There's no satisfaction now. No quiet thrill of pride, no happiness. There's…nothing.

When Randolph told me he didn't want to get involved with New Field, I was furious. Sharing that fury with Seraphina, letting her see me on the verge of losing control, wasn't an option. Had I just asked for time and space to process, she would have given it to me. Instead, I shut her out completely, reiterated my stupid rules and drove her away.

Just more evidence that her leaving was the best thing for both of us. She deserves someone who will be able to let down their guard, love her the way she loves so fiercely.

My fingers curl into fists in my pockets. The thought of her offering that love to someone else makes my vision blur. The possibility of her saying another man's name, of taking him to her bed and parting her legs for him—

I turn away from the window. The only reason I managed to survive on the streets was because I suppressed everything. I didn't think about the people Dominic, Cassian and I stole from as humans, I thought of them as targets. Not feeling helped us survive. I could function for the first time since the raspy echoes of Mom's final breaths, followed by that long, single beep, ended my childhood. Melanie's betrayal sealed my heart behind the walls I'd already started to build. I turned into someone cold, ruthless.

The door flies open. I whirl around, then growl as Dominic and Cassian saunter in.

"Whoa." Cassian holds up his hands. "Chill, bro."

"What are you doing here?"

Dominic raises one brow. "We were supposed to meet here for dinner?"

I grab the back of my neck and try to massage out some of the tension that's turned it into a stiff board. No luck.

"I forgot."

"You, Aiden Hawke, the most organized man in New York, forgot?" Cassian plops into my chair and puts his feet up on my desk, grinning when I glare at him. He glances down at my desk. I make it halfway across the room before he picks up the copy of the job listing.

"Executive assistant?"

I rip the paper out of his hand. "None of your concern. Are we going to dinner or what?"

"First," Cassian says as he rises and heads toward my liquor cabinet, "we're having a drink and you're telling us why you're suddenly in need of a new assistant."

"No."

Cassian ignores me as he pulls out three glasses and my most expensive brandy. Dominic slowly walks over, hands tucked casually in his pockets.

"Did you two have a fight?"

The quiet calm in his voice banishes my anger, leaving me empty once again.

"Not really a fight. Seraphina and I realized we weren't right for each other." I turn away and look back out over the city. "The engagement's off."

"Here." Cassian pushes a glass into my hand.

"Thanks."

I want to toss back the entire glass, want the burn of alcohol and the blessed mercy of forgetting for just a while. But I'm not about to cede control now when I need it the most.

"The New Field deal fell through. I pushed Seraphina away. She gave me back the engagement ring."

Dominic's eyes widen a fraction. The smallest gesture that speaks volumes for a man who is even more adept than I am at concealing his emotions.

"Yeah." My grin is humorless as I glance at Cassian. "I messed up. You were right. The engagement was fake. One of my clients threatened to walk if I didn't settle down. I had a big deal on the line with him, and once those photos hit the press, Seraphina agreed to help me." I raise my glass and take another drink. "Something changed between us. I got to see another side of her and I liked it. I liked it a lot."

Cassian snorts. "Like's not the word I would use."

"Well, you're not me," I snap back. "If I was capable of loving her back, I would."

Dominic puts a hand on my shoulder. "You care about her, Aiden."

"Of course I care." Dominic's rare display of affection unsettles me, makes me restless. "But caring isn't enough. Not for Seraphina. She deserves love."

Cassian brings the bottle over and tops off my glass. "So what, you don't love us?"

I roll my eyes. "We kept each other from starving and saved each other's lives more than once. We earned the respect we share. It's different."

"How?" Dominic pushes. "She worked herself like crazy for you for three years. You said yourself she made you a better advisor. And then she agrees to a fake engagement to help you."

"I saw the way she looked at you." The teasing tone is

gone from Cassian's voice, replaced by a seriousness I'm not used to. "And the way you looked at her.

"You know what I admired the most about you for so long? How strong you were. Even on the worst days when we were digging in the trash for food, you never flinched." Cassian's frown deepens. "But you've taken it too far. You don't have to do this on your own."

"My pain is private," I ground out. "I don't share. With anyone."

"You shared with Seraphina," Dominic says quietly.

"And that was a mistake," I retort. "She's already been through hell. I have no right to ask her to stay with me when I'm incapable of being what she needs."

"Did she ever ask you to change?" Cassian demands. "Did she walk away after Randolph pulled out, or did you push her away?"

I blink. My heart starts pounding in my chest, thundering against my ribs.

"I..." My breath rushes out. "She offered me time. Space. Whatever I needed. But I didn't want her to get pulled in."

The emotion I've been suppressing is starting to simmer, rise up. I try to keep it down, to maintain some semblance of control.

"She knows you, Aiden." Dominic approaches, stops behind Cassian. "Just like we do. We've always been here for you. And I imagine, if you gave her a chance, Seraphina would be, too."

"But you didn't even give her a choice." Cassian throws up his hands and stalks back to his chair, dropping down into it a frustrated exhale. "And is that because you're protecting her or protecting yourself?"

The accusation hits me square in the chest. I stare at

him, the words penetrating my shield. Every time I pushed Seraphina away, she gave me space. Time to deal with my demons while never wavering from my side. She saw me, all of me, and instead of letting her in, I gave in to fear and pushed her away.

"That's one of the things I love about Aiden..."

When Seraphina said those words in front of George Randolph in Venice, the way she looked at me, I knew. Deep down I knew she wasn't just acting for Randolph's sake. And I knew the feelings she stirred inside me weren't fleeting. No, they were feelings I've been fighting for far too long.

My lips part. "I'm in love with Seraphina."

Cassian throws up his arms. "Finally." He points at Dominic. "You owe me fifty bucks."

I glare at them. "You bet on me being in love?"

"Oh, we both knew you were." Dominic pulls out his wallet and slowly starts pulling out ten-dollar bills. "Cassian just bet we could get you to say it out loud before dinner."

I'm in love with Seraphina. I'm in love with the assistant who saw my passion and did everything she could to help my firm grow. I'm in love with the fire dancer who wields flames with confidence. And I'm in love with the woman who once thought she was broken and, instead of locking herself away, rebuilt herself piece by piece. She's not perfect, but I don't need her to be. I just need her to be who she's always been.

I need to talk with Seraphina. Need to tell her how I feel, how sorry I am. She may take one look at me and tell me to go to hell. But I need to take this chance. Need to know I did everything I could to show her I love her and, God willing, win her back.

CHAPTER SIXTEEN

Seraphina

Three days later

THE TEMPLE OF DENDUR is small, with a gateway made of sandstone and the small sanctuary located just behind it. But its size doesn't make it any less impressive. Papyrus and lotus plants are carved into the base of the temple. The interior of the sanctuary is softly lit, golden light bathing over the ancient stone. The reflecting pool surrounding the temple makes it easy to imagine such a temple sitting just beyond the banks of the Nile.

A stark contrast to the soaring glass wall to my right that faces Central Park. I still can't believe I'm dancing at the Metropolitan Museum of Art. Jessica called me on Tuesday, her excitement so intense it took several times of me encouraging her to slow down before she finally shared that a benefactor had not only booked the entire exhibition wing at the Met, but had also sold an additional two hundred seats for the show.

My heart twists in my chest as I glance at my reflection in the mirror set up in one of the makeshift dressing rooms. I'm wearing the same outfit I wore that night at the Hudson Springs gala: red halter with sparkling sequins, black skirt and a red rose tucked behind one ear. Unlike that night, however, I'm not wearing a wig or a mask. It's just me, Seraphina Clark.

I've spent the last couple of days deep-cleaning my apartment and the nights curled up with old movies. Tuesday was spent sending out résumés and scouring more job boards. I have an interview next week with a bank, but until I have an actual offer in hand, I'm going to keep applying. My savings will carry me for another couple months.

That, and I need the distraction. The focus of work so I can stop thinking about Aiden so much.

My hand goes to the chain around my neck. I gently tug and pulled the engagement ring free from the bodice of my halter top. It arrived by courier yesterday, along with a note.

"It was meant for you."

After a solid ten minutes of crying, I shut it away for a day inside my desk drawer. Just looking at it reminds me of Aiden in the dressing room of the store, his hand wrapped around mine as he slid it onto my finger.

But after a day of cleaning and a night of watching Anthony Andrews risk his life to save his estranged wife in *The Scarlet Pimpernel*, I woke up craving something, anything that would let me feel closer to Aiden. A man who, like the hero of one of my favorite movies, concealed his true self from the world even as he does what he can to make his portion of it better.

I found a necklace I'd purchased in college, a long silver chain with a small pendant, and swapped it out for the ring. One day I'll stop wearing it. One day the grief will be more of a companion than a cloud shadowing almost every aspect of my life.

I rub my thumb over the emerald. Release a shuddering breath. I miss him. I miss him like I've never missed anyone. It feels like my heart is missing a piece I'll never get back. I have to remind myself daily I'm whole, enough, without him in my life.

But God, it doesn't feel like it right now.

"Ready?"

I whirl around. Jessica's standing behind me, a smile on her face. She looks stunning in a long red gown that, rather than contrast with her own vivid red hair, makes it shine.

I tilt my head to one side. There's something off, though. A tension shimmering around her, faint lines by her eyes.

"I am. You all right?"

She waves a hand. "Just nerves. It's a big night for Cirque Obsidian. Way bigger than I expected."

"Fair. But what an accomplishment."

"Right?" She reaches out and grabs my hand. "I can't thank you enough for making sure Obsidian got some press. We wouldn't be performing here tonight without it."

At least something good came from all of this. I pull the necklace off and tuck it inside a pocket inside the nude shorts underneath my skirt. Breathe out before I walk to the door. "Okay. Let's do this."

"You're going to do great."

Jessica pulls me into a hug. I hesitate, then hug her back. She's the first true friend I've made since I put Brett behind bars. A positive to latch on to, lean into over the next few months as I work through my loss.

"Thanks." I glance down the hall. Techno music blasts. The silk performers. "I sound like I'm five asking this, but are my parents here?"

"Front row."

"Okay." I smile as I squeeze her hand. "I'm crazy nervous, but I'm excited."

"Would it make me sound like a patronizing big sister if I tell you how proud I am of you?"

God, I can't cry now. Not with eye shadow and liner and mascara on.

"No, it doesn't make you sound patronizing." I look up at the ceiling several stories above, blink rapidly and swallow past the lump in my throat. "Now stop talking before I walk out looking like I'm ready for Halloween."

We walk out of the dressing area and down a curtained-off hallway that leads to the stage. Jessica hands me my staff. When the silk performers' song concludes, she walks out. She asked if I wanted to dedicate my performance to anyone. It took me a day to think on it, to work up the courage to say what was on my heart.

"Our next performer has dedicated her dance to someone who made a big impact on her life. Who lifted her up and made her realize you can love again."

The crowd erupts into applause. The lights dim. I walk out onto the stage and take my place. The music starts, soft drops of melody that wash over me. Golden lighting fills the stage as I begin my dance. Gentle vocals fill the museum. I melt into the familiar tune, ease into my routine as I reach out to the darkened audience, let my heartache show on my face as I pull back, curl into my chest and slowly slide to the floor.

I think of Aiden as I arch up, each movement echoing the pain of getting back up after loss. The strains of violins pitch up as I cross to the candelabra flickering on the edge of the stage. I dip one end of the staff into the flames, then the other end.

The chorus bursts in with a swell of violins and cellos. The techno beats pulse inside me, mimicking my heartbeat as I roll the staff down my back, catch it and toss it into the air. The thrill of being in love, of realizing how much Aiden saw me and didn't pull away. He built me up, empowered me. In his own way, he cared for me.

The song swells. I wrap the staff around my shoulders, behind my back, across my chest. The fire flares. Then, slowly, I sink to the floor, the staff still burning in my hands as I lower my head.

Silence falls. A split second later the room erupts into wild applause. I force a small smile as I stand and give a slight bow.

My final goodbye to Aiden and everything he did for me. Maybe after tonight, I'll start to feel some peace.

I walk off the stage. Jessica's waiting for me. She wraps me in another hug and squeezes tight.

"Killed it." She pulls back and wipes away a tear of her own. "Absolutely killed it."

"Thank you."

She grabs my arm as I start to walk down the hall. "Do you mind hanging out for a moment?"

I want to just go back to the dressing room and sink into a chair. But I nod. Jessica walks back out into the spotlight.

"Absolutely incredible. Thank you, Seraphina. And now, before our next performance, please welcome our generous benefactor who made tonight's venue possible."

She walks toward me. The tension is back, as are the faint lines by her eyes as she stops next to me and looks back toward the stage. The lights dim. I can see a shadow moving against the dark.

Then the lights come up. My heart pitches straight down to my feet.

Aiden.

"Good evening." It's only been four days, but the sound of his deep, rich voice is like a balm to a wound. "I just wanted to take a moment to say thank you for coming out to support Cirque Obsidian and their artists." The audience claps as he smiles. "As some of you may know, I had a chance to see some of their performers in action recently at the Hudson Springs Botanical Gardens."

Quiet laughter sweeps through the crowd.

"But I want to highlight the impact Cirque Obsidian makes outside their studio. They don't just perform at galas and fundraisers. They offer free classes and performances at domestic violence shelters like Grace's Refuge, lead workshops for at-risk youth and detention centers, visit local hospitals."

The audience is silent now, their attention riveted on the man on the stage.

"An important woman in my life introduced me to just how big an impact Cirque Obsidian makes on our community. So tonight, for those of you inclined to support this group, the Hawke Foundation will not only match tonight's donations, but double the final amount."

Thunderous applause breaks out. I stare at Aiden, at

this man I once thought to be cold and unfeeling. Pride swells as he bows his head. Jessica walks out to him and shakes his hand. He waits until the applause dies down before he speaks again.

"The foundation's commitment is inspired by Seraphina Clark, a woman who has taught me about following one's heart and the value of not just giving, but giving with intention."

Hope—wonderful, terrible hope—blooms in my chest.

"Enjoy the show."

He nods to the audience. And then his gaze latches on to me. My breath catches in my chest at the sheer emotion burning in his eyes. He walks off the stage toward me, his steps strong and sure. I stand rooted to the spot, my heart pounding so hard I feel like I might pass out.

He stops in front of me.

"Seraphina."

"Aiden." I bite down on my lower lip. "That was beautiful."

"Thank you."

His hand comes up, as if he's going to touch me. But he stops, lets his arm drop back to his side. My hope quivers.

"Your performance…" He stops, his eyes locked on to mine as he breathes in deeply. "It was perfect."

"Thank you." I gesture to the stage. "You arranged all this?"

"I did. With the stipulation I be allowed to speak after your performance."

My hands tighten on my staff. I don't know what to do, what to say. I can't imagine another reason for why he's here. But a part of me is still afraid, so afraid it's not what I think, that I'm dreaming and I'll wake up any second.

"Is there somewhere we could talk?"

I nod, not trusting myself to speak. I turn and walk down the hall, every single cell in my body attuned to his presence behind me. His scent wraps around me, makes me want to stop and throw myself into his arms.

I lead the way out of the glass hall to a nearby stairwell. We climb up, exiting out onto the rooftop garden Jessica reserved for a post-performance reception. Cocktail tables are draped in ivory cloth and scattered amongst the statues. Votives flicker in the dimming light. Sculpted evergreens and tall grasses sway gently in the summer breeze as the sun sets, painting the sky with strokes of violet, rose, orange.

I move to one of the tables, my body trembling. When I finally look back at Aiden, his eyes fix on me once again with an intensity that sucks the air from my lungs.

"I missed you."

My throat closes. "I missed you, too." I shake my head. "A part of me will always miss you, Aiden."

"See, it's not that easy for me." He takes a step toward me. Just one, but my pulse stutters. "It's not just a part of me. It's all of me."

He continues his advance. The emotion in his eyes draw me in, hypnotize me with their intensity. Desire, yes, but longing, too, and something I want so desperately to be real I'm afraid I'm imagining it.

He stops in front of me, just a few inches away.

"The hardest part," he murmurs as his hand comes up again and he captures a strand of hair between his fingers, "was realizing I've been in love with you for years."

The hope I'd been battling takes over, fills me until I feel like I'm walking on air as I gaze up at the man I love.

"Years?" I finally choke out.

"Years." His other hand comes up and he cups my jaw, runs his thumb along my cheek. "Please tell me I didn't realize it too late."

I smile up at him as the tears I've been fighting off and on all night finally win and stream down my cheeks.

"It's never too late—"

He cuts me off with a soul-searing kiss. His lips slant across mine, his kiss demanding and possessive. I respond to his need, throw my arms around his neck as I press myself against him. One arm clamps down around my waist, pulls me even closer against his body. I don't know where I end and he begins.

He lifts his head and slides his fingers into my hair, presses my face against his throat.

"God, Seraphina, I almost lost you."

"I'm here," I murmur against his skin. "I'm right here, Aiden."

He pulls back, trails his fingers from my temple to my jaw. "I don't deserve you."

"Aiden—"

"I mean it, Seraphina. You gave me everything and I took it without giving anything in return."

"Stop." His eyes widen in surprise, and I place a finger over his lips. "I will tell you this over and over until you finally believe it. You are so much more than you believe yourself to be. And you saw me, truly saw me." I graze my fingers over the faint stubble on his jaw, then up to his dark hair. Smile faintly as his eyes close and he leans into my touch. "It frightened me, how easily you could read me, how you paid attention to the little things even as you claimed you weren't good at relationships."

"I never wanted one. Not," he adds as he gently brushes his nose against mine, "until you."

"I've had a crush on you for years." I laugh when he arches a brow. "I told myself it was just a harmless crush. That's why I always called you Mr. Hawke. It was a reminder to myself you were off-limits."

His shuddering breath fills the space between us.

"The night you left, I told myself I made the right choice." He scoffs. "I was lying to myself. My past shaped me into a cold, calculating shadow of the man I once thought I would be. It was so much easier to choose distance over getting emotionally involved and potentially losing someone else I care about."

"I understand. I do," I insist as he lifts his head to look at me. "It's understandable, Aiden. You've been through hell. I held myself back, too, remember?"

His mouth softens into a genuine smile. "Yes, but then you saw me, all of me, and still looked at me the way you did. Do you have any idea," he murmurs as he brushes a finger over my lower lip, "how terrifying it is to realize someone sees all of your flaws and still wants to be with you? To wonder if one day they'll wake up and realize it's too much, or that you're going to eventually let them down, too, and that maybe they would just be better off without you?"

I shake my head. "I'm not."

"Dominic and Cassian told me the same thing."

I let out a half laugh. "Both of them?"

"Both of them," Aiden repeats, his tone decidedly unamused. "They ambushed me the day after you left. Annoyed me plenty, but it was also a good conversation. One in which I realized I haven't been in control for a very long time. I used control as a way to avoid pain. I take risks every day with the work I do, but I wasn't willing to put my own heart on the line."

He steps back, his hands sliding down to capture mine.

"I came tonight because I needed you to see I'm capable of changing. Of being vulnerable and letting people into my life."

"You certainly did that," I say with a smile.

"When I saw you dance, I thought I'd lost you."

I shake my head fiercely. "No. I… I wanted to honor what we had. What you gave me."

"You inspire me." He raises my fingers to his lips, lays the gentlest of kisses on my knuckles. "It took my brothers knocking me over the head with the obvious, but you showed me the power of trusting those who care about me. How to let them in." He smiles. "You were right, you know. I called Randolph after they left."

Anticipation surges. "And?"

"I told him about David. He's on board with the New Field proposal on the condition you and I oversee it. Together."

"Oh, Aiden. That's incredible."

"And possible because of you." His smile dims. "I'm offering myself to you, Seraphina, wounds and all. I want to be with you more than I've ever wanted anything in my life. And," he adds before I can say anything, "I want a future with you."

He's offering me so much. Yet one last barrier still lingers, threatening to derail our reunion.

"I want that with you, too, Aiden."

"But?"

I want so badly to say I'll take whatever he's offering. But I can't. We both deserve the future we want.

"I told you before that having a family was a nonnegotiable for me."

He nods. "I've done a lot of thinking about that over the last few days. You were afraid I would think differently of you after you shared your story. I didn't realize I'd been holding on to a similar fear." He reaches up and cups my face. "Yet you accepted me."

I turn my head and press a kiss to his palm. "Yes."

"I will always carry some guilt for what happened to David. But just like I had choices, so did he." His throat bobs as he swallows hard. "And my father chose to hurt us. I can choose not to repeat the past."

My chest heaves as I draw in a shuddering breath. "Does that mean..."

"I meant what I said on stage, Seraphina. One of the things I admire about you is your kindness, your compassion. You gave back to the shelter that supported you. You give with intention. You inspire me to do the same, to be a better person." He lowers his head, presses his forehead against mine the way he did during the photo shoot. "When I'm with you, I can see myself being a good husband. A good father."

The last threat lurking just beyond our happiness evaporates.

"Are you sure?" I ask.

"I'm terrified," he says with a slight grin, "but cutting off the possibility of having a family was just another avoidance. Starving myself of any connections to keep myself safe. I'm done living my life that way. When

I think about the kind of parent my mother was, the kind of father John could have been if I'd let him in sooner..."

His voice trails off as his eyes grow distant. Then he shakes his head. "I'm finally starting to accept that regret. When I thought about Mom and John and what they did for me, I realized I wanted to have the chance to be even half the kind of parents they were. But," he adds with another kiss to my fingers, "it's your choice. It's always your choice."

I close the gap between us, lay one hand over his chest. The steady thump of his heart beneath my palm fills me with joy.

"I choose you, Aiden. Always."

"Then before I kiss you senseless..."

He drops to one knee.

"Seraphina Clark, would you do me the honor of being my wife?"

The tears are pouring down my cheeks. I smile through them, nod my head as I try to choke out a "yes."

"Do you still have the ring?"

I step away and wipe at my cheeks with the backs of my hands as I pulled my skirt to one side and reach into my pocket. I slide the ring off the chain and place it in his palm, much like I did just a few nights ago. But tonight, instead of grief and heartache, there's love. Love and a happiness so incredible I feel like I might burst.

"I asked your father for your hand tonight."

My mouth drops open. "What?"

"I asked Jessica to introduce us. Your mother likes me. Your father threatened to drop me off on some obscure Midwestern highway if I ever hurt you again. And then he gave me his blessing." He nods toward the ring in his hand. "May I?"

He slides the ring onto my finger, his eyes reverent as he looks up at me. "Even before I could admit to myself that I was in love with you, I chose the emerald for you."

I gaze down at the ring, glittering up at me as if celebrating that it's back where it belongs. And then I look at Aiden as he rises and cups my face once more in his hands. The man who did one of the most incredible acts of love and vulnerability I've ever seen just to show me he wanted to try.

"I love you, Aiden."

"And I love you, Seraphina." He leans down, kisses my brow. "Now, I believe I promised I was going to kiss you senseless."

His kiss is everything, full of desire and love and a promise so sweet I can hardly believe the turn my life has taken. I performed my dance tonight thinking it was a goodbye.

But now, as Aiden whispers his love against my lips, I know our future is just beginning.

EPILOGUE

Aiden

Five years later

WAVES RUSH UP the golden beach of Bibione before retreating back into the Adriatic Sea. The shushing of the water kindles distant memories of running up and down the sand, giggling as my parents chased me on one of our only vacations to the Jersey Shore.

The memory is bittersweet, one of the few happy ones that includes my father. But instead of shoving it away, I embrace it, latch on to the tiny details I suppressed for so long. The warmth of the sand beneath my feet. The sweet scent of Mom's perfume.

"Daddy!"

I turn, a big smile spreading across my face as Shaun runs across the beach as fast as his three-year-old legs will carry him. I crouch down and open my arms, a laugh escaping as my son throws himself against my chest.

"Are you enjoying the beach?" I ask as I stand up with him clinging to me like a spider monkey.

"Yup!" he replies with a big grin. "I love sand."

I run my hand through his thick brown curls, grimacing at the granules of sand that shower down over his shoulders.

"I noticed."

I smile when I see my wife slowly walking toward us. More like waddling, although I'll never tell her that. Seraphina's pregnancy with Shaun had been textbook-perfect. But this one has challenged her. Small wonder given that she's carrying two babies this time instead of one.

"I think he's gotten faster," she says, her voice slightly breathless as she reaches us.

Her stomach is round even though she still has four months to go The wind catches her hair and pulls loose strands of gold across her face. Dark half-moons are etched in the fragile skin beneath her eyes.

She's stunning. Gorgeous. Possessiveness grips me as her hand slides down to her stomach.

"And how are you?" I ask my wife as I stand with Shaun wrapped safely in my arms.

Her tired smile lights up her face as she stops in front of me. "Tired but happy."

"You could have stayed back at the villa," I murmur as I cup her face and run my thumb across her cheek.

Seraphina nods toward Shaun, who's happily splashing in the waves. "And miss this?"

I grin as Shaun lands on his rear and lets out a delighted squeal. "Fair point."

Seraphina leans into me. I pull her closer, savor the heat that burns just as bright and hot as it did that night our eyes met at the gala.

"Daddy!" Shaun squeals. "You kissed Mommy!"

I lift my head and smile down at my wife. "I did." I turn to my son, drop a kiss on his button nose. "Because I love your mother very much."

"I love her, too!"

"As you should." I kiss my son once more before looking back at my wife and smiling. "She's incredible."

Seraphina's smile fills me. My wife, mother of my children, and my partner. Hawke Financial is thriving, thanks in no small part to her continued work as my head of client services. A promotion that took over a year—and hours spent in bed—to convince her to accept. Her attention to detail and superior communication have made our clients feel even more valued.

Clients like Senator George Randolph. He lost his first campaign, but he kept his promise on the New Field proposal. It took a year, but we finally flipped the board and ousted Victor Hale. Randolph nominated several candidates he trusted to the board while serving as the face of the campaign against New Field and everything they'd done to hurt the prisoners entrusted to their care. His follow-through despite his political loss led to his being named as the face of prison reform and a successful comeback in last year's election.

"What's that smile for?"

I look down at my wife. "Where to start?"

Her green gaze softens. I'm grateful that while our son has inherited my hair and smile, he took after his mother and grandmother with his vivid green eyes.

"We're pretty lucky," she agrees as she leans into my embrace.

I drop a kiss on her forehead and glance over at the sea. We married in Venice four years ago in the Palazzo Pisani

Moretta. Dominic and Cassian served as my groomsmen, and David did me the honor of being my best man. A week after I proposed to Seraphina at the Met, I flew to South Carolina to visit him. We talked for hours on the beach, sharing our mutual guilts and hardships at moving on from our pasts. When I left, he came with me to meet Seraphina, who welcomed him with open arms. He's even come with us to Italy a few times after I purchased a small villa just outside of Venice. I have my brother back, thanks to the quiet patience and encouragement of my wife.

I gaze out over the water. Out of all the trips we've taken, this one is my favorite. Not just for visiting the place my mother dreamed of, but for finally easing the grief with happy memories.

Hawke Financial will be waiting for us when we return. So will Grace's Refuge, where Seraphina and I both now volunteer. After the showcase at the Met, she offered an exclusive interview to a different magazine about why Grace's Refuge and Cirque Obsidian were so important. She donated her check to another women's shelter in the city. That it was a rival magazine of *Gilded* still makes me smile.

She still dances, too, performing several times a year for Obsidian. She insists she will get me to try a fire dancing class one day, although she thankfully paused on classes during her pregnancy. I love watching my wife dance, love seeing her increasing skill and confidence. But the protective side of me is also very glad she's taking a break.

I wrap an arm around Seraphina's waist and pull her closer, my hand settling on the side of her swollen belly.

"I love you," I murmur against her hair.

"I love you, too," she whispers back.

Beneath my hand, the babies shift. New life waiting to burst into this world. And I know, as I stand on the beach with my wife and son in my arms and our future children beneath my fingertips, that choosing Seraphina and giving her the chance to choose me is the best decision I ever made.

* * * * *

Did My Fiancée Promotion *sweep you off your feet? Then you're sure to love the second installment in the Forbidden Bosses trilogy, coming soon. In the meantime, check out these other stories from Emmy Grayson!*

Deception at the Altar
Still the Greek's Wife
Pregnant Behind the Veil
Enemy in His Boardroom
Wed for the Headlines

Available now!